Sue blurted, "Ted said he'd give up the custody battle if you and I stopped living together."

The silence that followed dragged on for what seemed a long time. Alex stopped mopping her brow with the small kitchen towel and sat perfectly still. Her face registered no surprise. "I guess I expected this to happen," she remarked.

"Nothing's happened."

"Not yet." Alex rose from her chair.

"Don't run from me, Alex." Sue ached inside. For the first time in years she was satisfied with her life and now she was being forced to make an impossible choice.

"I'm not." Alex smiled bleakly. "What about the house you wanted to look for?"

Sue shrugged helplessly. "He's offering me Cassie."

STICKS and STONES

•JACKIE•
CALHOUN

The Naiad Press, Inc.
1992

Printed in the United States of America on acid-free paper
First Edition

Edited by Christine Cassidy
Cover design by Pat Tong and Bonnie Liss
    (Phoenix Graphics)
Typeset by Sandi Stancil

Library of Congress Cataloging-in-Publication Data

Calhoun, Jackie.
    Sticks and stones / by Jackie Calhoun.
        p.   cm.
    ISBN 1-56280-020-5
    I. Title.
PS3553.A395S75   1992
813'.54--dc20   91-38104
                                                          CIP

In loving memory of
Janet S. Calhoun,
who also wrote

With Heartfelt Thanks:

To Chris for unconditional faith in my writing ability. To my support group — Chris, Diane, Sandy — for reading as I write, for always being there when I need them.

To my daughters, Janny and Jessica, who gave me the enriching experience of motherhood and to Dick, who assisted and who should have been acknowledged in my second book. To the rest of my family: my sisters, Chris and Kay, and my cousin David. All of those mentioned are my roots and my branches, who make my writing possible.

About the Author

Jackie Calhoun, who was born and grew up in Wisconsin, moved back to her home state in 1987 after spending twenty-seven years in Indiana. She is the author of *Lifestyles* and *Second Chance* and is now at work on her fifth novel.

I

Sorting through the papers on her desk, looking for lesson plans, Alex attempted to organize thoughts out of the panic in her mind. She had to put the fear behind her, because in less than five minutes her next class would begin. Already kids were sauntering through the open door, greeting her. She failed to recall names she had learned weeks ago. Momentarily closing her eyes, she took a deep breath and gathered her resources. Forget the damn letter, she told herself, deal with it later.

While the students restlessly exchanged comments at their desks, Alex started to close the door and was startled when Lisa Gavinski stuck her head in the opening. Knowing that the other teacher had received a copy of the letter, Alex forced a smile. "Anything I can do, Alex, just ask. Okay?" Lisa offered, giving Alex the thumbs-up sign.

Alex nodded. "Thanks." She watched Lisa continue down the hall, then closed the door.

Earlier she had been called to the principal's office where Davidson had handed her a copy of the letter. Since then she had been unable to concentrate on her students or classes. Alex wondered if she only imagined that the kids knew. Pulling herself together with a deep sigh, she faced her fourth hour class and launched into a lecture that failed to interest her. So how could it interest them? she wondered. And as if in confirmation, Billy James hooted from his back row seat.

"You have a comment, Billy?" Raising her eyebrows in question, she fixed the long-haired boy with a cool stare.

"No, ma'am. I was just remembering a joke."

"Try to concentrate on history. I know it's difficult but give it a go, will you?"

"Yes, ma'am. Sorry."

When she had first come to this small school, she had been insulted when the boys called her ma'am; she was much too young for that appellation. Now she knew they were just being polite, deferring to her position of authority. The kids had never been her enemies. She was sympathetic to what was important to them and always offered them a ready ear. She was ashamed now to look at them askance, wondering if any of them were responsible for or had knowledge of the letter.

She opened her mouth to ask Billy to tell her the joke during detention, but remembered she had softball practice after school. The day was going to be endless.

After school, during practice, Alex batted the ball to the fielders. This gave her some idea of their skill level, which was a little discouraging because they missed or dropped most of her hits, but the fresh warm air blew away the film of distaste the letter had deposited in her. She worked forty-five minutes on fielding, forty-five minutes on batting, then matched her pitchers with catchers to practice.

When she climbed into her Chevy S-10 truck and headed home, she couldn't recall much of the day. What she remembered, as she slumped on the couch, was the letter that held her in a relentless rage.

She failed to hear the key in the door lock and jumped when Sue entered carrying two grocery bags. Alex took one and set it on the kitchen counter.

Sue grinned. "So, how you doing, babe?" Her eyebrows arched in question. "Not so good?"

Alex looked into the large, soft brown eyes with relief. Here was succor. "Better, now that you're home. You can tell?"

"Drapes drawn, no lights, no TV or radio, just you by yourself. How come?" Sue peeked into one of the bags and started removing the contents.

"Where's Cassie?" Alex asked.

"With her dad." Leaning on tiptoes toward her, Sue kissed her. "How about a hug?"

Sighing, Alex wrapped her arms around Sue and returned the kiss, then handed her the letter.

"What's this?" Sue scanned the paper and scowled. "What the hell." She glanced at Alex.

"Read it. I think I'm behaving pretty well, considering." Looking over Sue's shoulder, she read with her.

Sue turned, her eyes dark and troubled, and met Alex's gaze. "This is your worst nightmare come true."

Alex laughed humorlessly. "Isn't it?"

Sue gestured angrily with the letter. "Do you know who wrote this?"

Alex shrugged and smiled grimly. "Someone who doesn't like me very much?"

"And someone who knows us," Sue added.

Nodding, Alex propelled Sue to the couch.

The typewritten letter, wrinkled and limp, lay face up on the cushion between them.

Alex Sundstrum, a teacher at Plankton High School, lives in a practicing homosexual relationship with another woman and her child. Miss Sundstrum teaches and coaches impressionable girls. She should not hold a position where she can influence or corrupt students. If this woman continues teaching and coaching, this matter will have to be taken to the press.

"Want me to show it to Ted?" Sue asked. Ted, a local attorney, was Sue's ex-husband.

"Not really." Alex felt the anger stir again. The letter was signed *A Disturbed Parent*. Whoever wrote it was disturbed all right, she thought, and said as much.

Sue snorted a laugh.

"So, how was *your* day?" Alex asked. Sue worked as a guidance counselor at the high school in the

4

town where they lived, Chancelor, ten miles from where Alex taught.

"We're not through discussing yours."

Alex's voice shook. "I don't think I've ever been so furious. Everybody got a copy, Sue — the faculty, the administration, the school board members. I feel like somebody took my clothes off in front of everyone. You know?"

"I know," Sue replied softly. She touched Alex's hair, then caressed the side of her face with the back of one hand.

"Want to go to bed?" Alex asked as a surge of desire swept through her. She yearned to forget herself in Sue's soft curves.

"I think we need to talk," Sue insisted.

Alex said, "If all those other people knew, the kids will know next."

"Oh, Alex, they know anyway."

"You talk like I have a big *L* on my forehead," Alex remarked, getting up to answer the phone.

A woman's voice quavered in her ear. "You're not fit to teach, you know that?"

"Who is this?" she asked angrily.

The voice became shrill. "You're a pervert. Best thing you could do is quit."

Alex slammed the phone on its cradle. Vomit crept up her throat as her heart hammered and her legs grew weak.

"What is it? Who was it?"

Alex repeated the woman's words.

"Oh, Alex," Sue said, putting her arms around her. "Don't believe it. What does she know? You're a wonderful teacher. You're good with the kids. You're good for them. You've got to know that."

5

Alex impatiently brushed away tears. "Do you think the newspapers would print it, maybe as a letter to the editor?"

"No, I don't think the newspapers will touch it. You want me to talk to the attorney who did my divorce tomorrow?"

Alex nodded, momentarily so hurt she felt defeated. "Wouldn't do any harm, I guess." Then, looking for escape, she said, "Let's go to bed."

Sue hesitated before shrugging compliance.

Once there, though, Alex found it difficult to become aroused or concentrate.

"It's okay, Alex. Let's just forget it for now," Sue murmured, lightly scratching Alex's back with both hands. "You are so slender."

Alex knew how Sue struggled to keep her five-foot-three-inch frame under one hundred and thirty pounds. She caressed the silky skin, working herself into a state of desire. "I love you just the way you are. I don't like skinny women."

"That's why you keep yourself that way, right?" Sue's closed lids flew open when Alex gave her a decidedly passionate kiss. "I thought we gave up on this."

"You gave up on it." Rolling onto her side and pulling Sue closer, Alex ran one hand down her back and between her legs.

"Mmm. You do that so well," Sue said, deftly working her fingers into Alex, stroking gently.

The next morning, Alex awakened, ravenous, as the blinds lightened in the first rays of daylight. "How about a shower and some breakfast, sweetie?"

Curled up against Alex's side, Sue buried her

face under Alex's arm and mumbled. "What time is it?"

Alex lifted her head to look at the clock. "Just before five." Sliding an arm under Sue, she held her close for a few minutes.

"Give me another hour of sleep. Okay?"

"Okay, sweetie." Alex freed her arm and rolled out of bed. "I'm gonna run then. I'll be back at six."

Spring gave Alex energy. She remembered the taste and feel of winter, how breathing had pinched her nostrils and frozen her lungs, recalled the long months of icy, silent sterility. She ran through the newly dawning day with light feet and head, intoxicated with the season — the blooming trees and bushes, the greening grass, the birds singing their heads off.

The soft thudding of her tennis shoes and her harsh breathing joined the sounds of the morning. Shades of red spread across the blue of the eastern sky. Down by the river, which mirrored the colors of the promising day, she picked up the footpath along the bank near the marina. Lisa Gavinski caught up with her in the next half mile and they matched pace.

Lisa, after applying for the varsity softball coaching position and losing out to Alex, coached the junior varsity team. She stood a couple inches taller than Alex's five-foot-nine. She had a baby face and enormous blue eyes, giving her an aura of innocent sweetness. "We meet again," she remarked with a small smile.

"So we do," Alex grunted. Feeling uncomfortable — *exposed* was the correct word — she ran on in silence. She thought Lisa must have slowed to stay with her.

Returning to the apartment, Alex tiptoed into the bedroom. Sue reached for her, pulled her onto the bed and into the softness of her arms, and kissed her with wonderfully warm lips.

"Is it cold out?" she murmured.

"It's nice." Moving closer, Alex said wistfully, "I could crawl right back in there with you."

"What time is it anyway?" Sue turned toward the clock.

"Six-fifteen. Time to get up. Want to shower with me?"

Sue heard Cassie close the door softly behind her and call, "Hi, Mama." Portable phone against her ear, Sue stuck her head out her bedroom door and waved to her daughter.

Cassie trudged into the bedroom and dumped her crumpled papers onto the double bed where her mother and Alex slept. She sorted through them as Sue, intent on the phone conversation, ran a hand over her daughter's head. Cassie resembled her father — dark brown hair, hazel eyes, rosy cheeks — but had a short, sturdy little body. Someday she would fight the calories as her mother did.

"See, Mama." She proudly held up some of her school papers.

Sue nodded and smiled, her attention divided between the lawyer on the phone and Cassie. She missed both points and had to ask the attorney to repeat hers.

"Just keep doing what you have been doing. I can't stress that too much, Sue. Remember, you're doing nothing wrong, legally or otherwise. The school administration has to support Alex's legal rights. Her job should not be affected by any of this. Her lifestyle is her own business."

"Thanks. We'll send you a copy of the letter. Okay? Then if anything else happens, we'll send the retaining fee."

Sue gathered Cassie to her. The small pudgy arms closed tightly around her neck. "Hi, baby. I missed you. How was your stay with Daddy?"

"Okay, Mama." She gave Sue a warm, sticky kiss.

Sue unclasped Cassie's arms and held her so that she could look at her. She pushed the straying dark locks behind Cassie's small ears and smiled into her daughter's eyes. "So tell me about everything."

"Everything what?" Cassie asked, handing her mother a crumpled piece of paper. "I wrote you a letter."

"Nice. I like the different colors each word has."

"Mama, when do I have a riding lesson?"

"Friday, I think." Sue selected a few of Cassie's papers to hang on the refrigerator.

"Daddy's picking me up after school Friday. We're going to Great America Saturday."

"That's nice, honey." Sue longed to hug her child possessively. "Our next weekend we'll do something exciting. Go change. Okay?"

Pulling off her jacket, Cassie disappeared from the room. "Daddy bought a kitten for me, Mama, and he's got a girlfriend," the small voice called.

For a brief moment Sue hated Ted. Because she had moved into this apartment with Alex where no pets were permitted, Sue had been forced to give her cat to her close friend, Brenda Jackson, who owned and ran a stable. Now she and Cassie saw Tabby only when Cassie took riding lessons. Tabby had turned into a barn cat, catching mice and other small animals with merciless efficiency. Once Sue had watched her former elegant feline eat a half-grown rabbit in five minutes flat. "He didn't even chew it. He swallowed it whole," she later told Alex with despair.

"Ted has a girlfriend," Sue informed Alex in bed that night.

"Really? Do you care?" Alex turned from the papers she had been grading to glance over her reading glasses at Sue, who was lying on her back with a paperback.

"No, of course not," Sue said.

"Cassie tell you that?"

"Yeah. He also bought her a kitten."

"Hmmm. Well, maybe we can move where we can have pets one of these days."

"How was school today? Really."

"I got through the day. Whenever I look at anyone now, I wonder if that person wrote the letter. It's tiring to be so suspicious. I hate it." Alex put the papers and her glasses on the floor next to the bed and curled up next to Sue.

"Going to sleep?"

"I think so. I was so tired yesterday and today. I could have fallen asleep anywhere, any time."

Escape, Sue thought, setting her book on the bed table and turning off the light. "How's softball practice?"

"Okay. The kids are coming along. If willingness does it, they'll be champions."

"That's good." Sue kissed Alex's forehead and turned on her side so they lay spoon fashion, Alex wrapped around Sue's backside.

"I've got two good pitchers."

"Lucky you."

"Well, maybe not. Ginger's parents have always been supportive, but Kelly, the other pitcher, may pass Ginger by. I'll have to start her if she does, and her mother's a bitch."

"Interesting."

"This woman acts like she hates me when Kelly isn't on the mound. She seems to think her kid should be playing all the time. And I'd like to ask Ben Gray to help me coach. He's offered. That's Ginger's dad."

"Well, that could make it difficult," Sue said.

"He'd probably be the first to say start the best girl."

"What do you want to do this weekend? Cassie's going to be with her dad."

"I've got a riding lesson Saturday. Want to go with me? That's something you could do with Cassie." Alex yawned.

"Oh, yeah, can't you just see me riding around with all those little kids. Horses scare me."

"You could ride with me, or Brenda would take you alone, I'm sure. She's got a soft spot for you and Cassie you could sink a truck in." Alex's body jerked, a sure sign she was falling asleep.

"I didn't know she had any soft spots."

"Shame on you."

"Just teasing. You know I love Brenda."

"I know." Alex breathed into Sue's hair. "Let's go to sleep. I'm exhausted."

II

The following morning Sue was called to the hospital at six-thirty to see a student who had attempted suicide, leaving Alex in charge of getting Cassie to school.

"What do you want for breakfast, kiddo?" Alex asked, looking her over with a practiced eye. "Your socks don't match. Close but not quite the same."

"Do I have to change them?" Cassie asked, staring at her legs.

"I think it might be a good idea. One's blue and one's green."

"Joey had on two different shoes yesterday."

"What did the kids say about that?" Alex studied the child with interest.

"Some of them laughed."

"Do you want them to laugh at you?"

"No." Cassie headed back down the hall to her bedroom.

"How about oatmeal?" Alex called after her.

"Okay," Cassie replied as she disappeared.

Alex smiled. Someone had to make sure Cassie was fed and dressed decently, had brushed her hair and teeth and washed her face before launching her toward kindergarten. She loved it when she was the person for that job.

Whenever she had free time, the letter took over her thoughts. It had become a festering wound, and she couldn't leave it alone. The response so far from those who had received a copy had surprised and heartened her. The principal had told her to ignore it, assuring her that he was doing just that. The superintendent had suggested she throw it away, had said he hadn't wanted to show it to her in the first place. One school board member had visited her room and offered support. The faculty had continued to be friendly.

She wondered if Sue was right. Did everyone know what she had tried so hard to hide all these years? Had she only been fooling herself? But the rage she had experienced when she first read the letter returned whenever she thought of it. She could neither throw it away nor ignore it. Somehow she had to discover who had written it.

She loved her job at Plankton High School, and had once remarked to Sue that it was frosting on the cake to be paid to do what she did. Laughing softly and bitterly, she stared unseeing at the papers on the desk in front of her, while her fourth-hour students studied in groups. Never again would she make such a stupid statement. Everything associated with the school had become tainted for her.

"Miss Sundstrum, ma'am?"

Startled, she looked up into Billy James's narrow, slate-gray eyes, took note of his set mouth. He was one of her nicer hoods. Underneath his tough exterior she discerned a fairly nice guy. "Yes, Billy?"

"I don't care about World War Two."

She fought her urge to laugh at this determined statement. What had she done to deserve this? Why her class? "What do you care about, Billy?"

"I care about fixing cars and building houses and welding and stuff like that."

"I see." Thinking furiously, she decided to lay the burden on the principal. "After class we'll go see if Mr. Davidson can help you learn what you want to learn, but until then please take your seat."

She watched the boy walk to his chair — a long-haired rebel, still uncertain and awkward in his youth. How brave to challenge the system, she thought with her new state of mind.

* * * * *

15

Alex kissed Sue awake Saturday morning. "Can't it wait?" Sue asked, being drawn reluctantly from a dream.

"Later. Time only for a shower and breakfast before we go to the barn. Come on, sweetie."

"You gotta be kidding," Sue protested. "What time is it?"

"Eight-thirty and look at all that sunshine and smell that breeze." The blinds moved and the light around them dazzled.

"Hurts," Sue muttered and squeezed her eyes shut.

"I'll have to go without you," Alex said, rolling toward the edge of the bed.

"I'm coming," Sue replied, just as Alex knew she would.

Brenda was deep in the barn when they went searching for her. The predominant smells were of horses and hay. They found her turning out horses.

"Hey, you two. Good to see you." Brenda, broad-shouldered and buxom, spoke in a booming voice. Her brown hair was cut short, and from the back it was easy to mistake her for a man. She covered her vulnerability with a brash act, fooling neither Sue nor Alex.

"You're a hard woman to track down," Sue remarked.

Brenda put an arm around Sue's shoulders and herded her toward the tack room. "Gonna ride?"

"Not me," Sue said. "I'll check up on Tabby and watch."

Alex saddled and bridled her schooling horse, Satan, while the three of them talked. She fished the letter out of her jeans pocket and handed it to Brenda, who bristled as she read.

"Who wrote this?" Brenda shook the letter, startling the horse. Satan snorted and drew back against the cross-ties.

"That's what we all want to know," Sue remarked dryly, leaning against a dusty wall.

"Let me know when you find out. I'll take care of whoever it is."

"I believe you would, too," Alex said, exchanging a smile with Sue.

Sue and Brenda followed Alex and the horse out of the barn. Satan's shoes clanked on the old cement aisles and he blew through his nose and wiped it on Alex's sweatshirt, leaving green streaks. "Gross," Sue said disgustedly.

The horse and humans blinked in the bright daylight. Tabby bounded toward them from high weeds and Satan shied, nearly pulling the reins from Alex's grasp. Sue started when the horse unexpectedly jumped sideways.

Brenda laughed. "Sixteen hands and he jumps from a cat."

Alex mounted easily. She gathered the reins and urged Satan toward the riding arena.

"Look at her," Alex heard Brenda say admiringly. "She's got all the leverage she needs. You know?"

Brenda perched on the top rail of the fence so that she could holler instructions to Alex. Settling on a bench, Sue leaned against the warm wall of the barn with Tabby on her lap.

Posting along the rail and then over ground poles, feeling Satan's powerful rhythm between her legs, Alex grinned. It was the best feeling she'd had all week. The animal surging forward in response to her leg cues gave her the illusion of control.

"Good," Brenda shouted. "Right diagonal and everything. Pick up a canter. Warm him up around the rail and then take those in and outs." The two small jumps were spaced for one and a half strides.

Satan picked up the right lead as he lifted himself into a canter. Riding high, Alex glanced down at the horse's shoulder. Her hands dropped and Satan came to a jarring stop. Alex sailed headfirst over the shoulder she had been looking at and, rolled into a ball, hit the dirt hard.

Brenda leaped from the fence into the arena. "Well, at least you know how to fall." And then she admonished, "You should always look ahead."

Alex picked herself up and brushed herself off, moving her shoulders and arms to make sure everything was in its right place.

Sue had jumped to her feet, spilling a surprised Tabby from her lap. The cat meowed plaintively. "You all right?"

"I'm okay," Alex replied, taking the reins from Brenda and remounting. The feeling of control was gone along with the high. She rode carefully the remainder of the hour.

Brenda clapped Sue and Alex on the back as they climbed into the little gray truck. "Say hello to Cassie. Tell her I'll see her next week."

"Were you scared?" Sue touched the dirt still on Alex's shoulder.

Alex turned and met Sue's gaze with a grin. "It happened too fast. What is scary is waiting for it to happen again. Want to go home?"

18

Alex climbed into the shower late in the afternoon and groaned as the spray removed some of the grime and soreness. "Come on under here with me." Moving to one side, she made room for Sue, then leaned forward to kiss her mouth, her neck, her breasts — circling the nipples with her tongue, lightly sucking them. Gently she grasped Sue's hips, pulling her closer, cupping the generous bottom in her hands, then reached further to the mound of dark hair.

Sue took Alex's face between her hands and returned the kiss, tracing Alex's lips with her tongue. She caressed the smooth muscled back and clasped the small tight hips.

Warm water beat on Alex's back as she moved her mouth down Sue's body, kissing what she had just touched with her hands. The skin felt so soft and warm she moaned a little and heard Sue's answering moan. Enclosing Sue's thighs with her arms, she stilled their trembling even as she spread them.

"I can't stand up any longer," Sue gasped over the pounding water. "Please, Alex, stop." She drew Alex to a standing position and kissed her softly, the kiss deepening as it lengthened. The water turned cold, temporarily ending their passion.

"Cold showers really do work, don't they?" Alex observed, rinsing quickly under the icy water, making way for Sue to do the same.

Sue shivered as she climbed out to be enclosed in a large towel by Alex, who dried her off as if she were a child.

* * * * *

19

In bed they began again. Both enjoyed the expectation of climax, the slow passionate climb to orgasm. For a few minutes they lay face to face in each other's arms, relishing the sensation of skin touching skin, lips gently tasting. As their kisses grew more intense, their hands began to move, idly stroking. The caresses became intimate, creating a warm sea of passion.

Sue made her way down the length of Alex's body — tasting, touching, kissing the smooth skin, the soft curves — until her tongue and fingers became engulfed in a flood of desire and joined Alex's rhythm. She heard Alex groan deep in her throat, felt Alex's arms close around her hips and pull her down. She gasped at the warm touch of tongue.

They moved together, the blood pounding through them. Then it was over and they struggled for breath, their heartbeats slowing.

Alex whispered, "Come here. I want to hold you."

They lay in close embrace, the room growing shadowy around them. Just before they slept, Alex reached down and pulled the sheet over their damp, cooling bodies.

The sound of the phone strode into Sue's dream and she fumbled for the receiver in the dark room.

"You pervert."

"I beg your pardon?" Sue said, her mind thick with sleep.

"You should resign."

"There are no perverts here." She slammed the phone down hard and Alex, who had come instantly awake at the word *perverts,* jumped.

"What a rotten way to wake up."

"You're telling me," Sue agreed grumpily. "Are you hungry?"

"Starved. What's there to eat?"

"Leftovers."

"Want to do it again?" Alex asked, covering Sue with her long, slim body.

"Pervert." Sue grinned.

"That's a fighting word," Alex warned, pinning Sue's arms to the bed.

They wrestled until they fell onto the floor in a heap, tangled in the bedding.

"We need to change the sheets anyway," Sue remarked.

"Hey, kiddo, how was your weekend?" Alex asked. Cassie stood inside the closed apartment door with her small suitcase clutched in both hands. "Here, let me help you with that." She took the overnight bag and carried it down the hall to Cassie's room.

The girl sniffed and sneezed. She looked crabby. Sue, who was helping her daughter remove her jacket, placed a hand on the warm forehead and Cassie pushed it away. Sue hated how the weekends Cassie spent with her father often ended, with Cassie questioning her mother's authority. It took days for the three of them to settle back into a normal routine.

"So what's wrong, sweetie?" She kissed the rosy cheek and felt the short arms close around her neck. Smiling, she returned the hug. "That's more like it. You hungry?"

Cassie nodded.

"Tell me what you did this weekend," Alex said, coming back into the room and sitting at the table with Cassie.

"Went to Great America. I screamed on The Demon," Cassie said solemnly.

"You're supposed to scream," Alex said just as seriously.

She set a bowl of warmed-up chili in front of the little girl and ran her hand over the tangle of Cassie's hair.

Cassie pushed the bowl away. "I don't want chili."

"It's chili or nothing," Sue replied in a too calm voice.

Cassie ate the oyster crackers off the top of the steaming bowl. "Daddy gives me whatever I want to eat."

Sue felt her temples throb. "I give you what's good for you," she countered, knowing it wasn't always true.

Alex stood and ran a soothing hand down Sue's back. "Cool it," she said softly.

"Jean is pretty. She's Daddy's girlfriend." Cassie stirred the chili around in the bowl with the spoon, then picked the kidney beans out one by one and ate them.

"Don't play with your food," Sue admonished, wondering what Jean looked like.

"Can't we have Tabby back?" Cassie turned, her face now stained red around the mouth, her eyes pleading.

"You know we can't have pets here," Sue reminded her.

"Let's move then. Daddy's buying a house in the country. He said I can live with him and Jean."

The throbbing in Sue's temples turned into a monstrous headache and she thought she might vomit. She felt as if she had already lost Cassie. She had feared Ted might seek primary custody and had been relieved when at first he had not contested the divorce agreement. "Do you want to live with Daddy and Jean?" she heard herself ask as if from a great distance.

"Daddy says you and Alex shouldn't sleep together," Cassie said, eyeing them both. "Why?"

"He didn't tell you why?" Sue asked coldly, her heart pounding with distress. At that moment she hated Ted more than she ever had, yet she knew she would throw herself at his feet if it would keep Cassie with her.

"How did he know we sleep together?" Alex asked, sitting down again at the table and looking intently at Cassie.

"He asked where we sleep. He said men and women should sleep together." Cassie studied them. "What's queer?"

Control yourself, Alex's look said, but Sue was focused on her daughter.

"Why?" Sue's voice was barely audible.

"Daddy said you and Alex were queer."

Sue sat down next to her daughter and explained that she and Alex loved each other and that's what Ted considered queer, while Alex stood nearby and listened. Sue could feel Alex's gaze traveling from her to Cassie and back again.

* * * * *

"I want to kill him," Sue remarked in bed that night. She looked spent after so much emotion.

"I bet you do," Alex said with a sideways glance. She put an arm around Sue but Sue wouldn't let herself be drawn close.

"He's going to try to take her away," Sue said in a low voice. "He's just been biding his time until he bought a house and met someone else. I think I've always known this would happen."

"Don't the courts usually side with the mother?" Alex asked, hoping Sue was fretting needlessly.

"They side with the parent who can give the child the best environment." Sue's arms were crossed and she looked as crabby as Cassie had earlier.

"Cassie's happy with us." A niggling worry began to grow. Her relationship with Sue could crumble under the weight of losing Cassie. She slid down into the bed and put an arm over Sue, wanting reassurance, but Sue had none to give.

Instead, Sue felt annoyance at what she considered Alex's obstinate refusal to see the obvious.

III

Sue collected Cassie from Kiddie Kare for the drive to Plankton for Tuesday's game. The name of the after-kindergarten day-care center irritated Sue whenever she saw it. How could children learn to spell when adults misspelled regularly?

She felt somewhat disloyal following Alex's team, especially when the students from Chancelor asked if she would watch them play. When the two teams played each other, she sat with the Chancelor parents and cheered for both sides, making herself equally unpopular.

Today Cassie's nose looked red and sore and her face was flushed, but she insisted that she felt fine. Besides, it was such a pretty day. How could sitting in the sun hurt anyone? Sue reasoned.

"Hi, Alex," Cassie called as she climbed the steps to the bleachers with her mother.

Alex looked up from taping one of the player's ankles. "Come here, Cassie."

The child dropped Sue's hand and ran to Alex where she stood suddenly shy in front of the dugout.

"Want to be our bat girl?" Alex asked, applying the last strip of tape.

"What's a bat girl?"

"The bat girl picks up the bats and equipment and stuff, keeps them together by the fence."

"I can do that," Cassie agreed. She ducked her head and rubbed a toe in the dirt when Alex introduced her to the players.

One of the catchers put a cap on the little girl's head and pulled the bill down over her eyes. "Now you look like one of the team." Cassie pushed the brim up, took the hat off, looked at it, and then put it back on.

"You're gonna do just fine, Cassie," Kelly assured her, tugging a sock and shoe on over the tape Alex had just smoothed in place. She patted Cassie on the back before trotting off to practice pitching to her catcher.

Cassie swiveled, sought her mother in the bleachers with her eyes and waved to her.

"Okay, girls, give me your best. That's all I want," Alex said to her players before sending the starters to their field positions. Ginger took her stance on the pitcher's mound.

Sitting among the parents behind home plate, Sue glanced at Kelly's mother, Nancy Westover, and noticed no change of expression, heard no comment. Perhaps Alex only imagined that Mrs. Westover got her nose out of joint when Ginger started instead of Kelly. Then her attention gravitated to her daughter and Alex.

She loved watching Alex coach. For some obscure reason it turned her on when Alex trotted to the coach's box off third base when her team was up to bat or when she paced outside the dugout while her kids were in the field.

The sight of Cassie's small figure totally immersed in the job of picking up bats and batter's helmets and lining them up along the fence behind home plate tugged at Sue's heart. So intent on doing a good job, Cassie would never see a bat flung in her direction or a speeding foul ball.

When the game went into extra innings, the late afternoon sun dipped behind clouds and a breeze cooled spectators and players alike. Watching her team in the field, Alex stood behind Cassie with her hands on the child's shoulders. Always conscious of Sue in the stands, Alex threw a brief look at her but Sue's eyes remained focused on the playing field. Cassie shivered under Alex's touch and wiped her nose on her sweatshirt. "Go ask your mom if she has a jacket for you, kiddo."

"I'm not cold," Cassie replied stubbornly, leaning against Alex's legs.

After the game, Alex talked to students and spectators. She put an arm around Cassie's shoulders, and when she felt the child's hand touch her leg in a silent reminder of her presence,

27

introduced her to Ginger's parents as the new bat girl.

"She does a good job," Kathy Gray remarked.

Cassie visibly puffed up with pride and gave them a smile.

Alex laughed, then turned to Ben. "Can I still take you up on your offer to help coach, Mr. Gray?"

"Sure can. Gotta call me Ben, though." Ben Gray, a small, lean man, grinned at Alex. "It'll give me something to do."

"As if you don't have enough to do already, huh?" Alex said. Then added, "Any help's appreciated."

From the stands Sue studied Cassie and Alex and experienced a strange mix of emotions. She felt a little resentful because Cassie hadn't returned to her, because she seemed to prefer being with Alex right now, even though Sue understood why. She wanted to stand with her daughter and Alex but knew it was better if she didn't, especially with the letter pointing an accusing finger at her relationship with Alex.

When Sue left the bleachers and joined them, the words came somewhat reluctantly. "Nice win, Alex."

"Mama, did you see me being the bat girl?" Cassie broke in, forgetting her manners.

"Yes, I saw you, Cassie."

"Alex said I did good."

"I know you did, honey."

Alex looked at Sue. "Want to eat out tonight?" she asked.

"Cassie has a cold."

"I'm very fine, Mama." Cassie jumped up and down in front of her mother.

"I'm talking to Alex, Cassie," Sue said.

"She has to eat somewhere. What difference does it make if we stop before going home?" Alex added, "I'll treat."

Frowning, knowing her resentment was misplaced, Sue put a lid on it with difficulty. "You don't have to treat. Where do you want to go?"

"The Good Place," Cassie shouted, walking backward and still jumping up and down.

"I wasn't asking you," Sue said.

"Why not? Why are you mad, Mama?"

"I'm not mad, but I'm talking to Alex and you keep interrupting."

"You are mad," Alex whispered in her ear.

Sue sighed.

"I want to ride with Alex," Cassie announced, staring defiantly at her mother.

"Go ahead," Sue said, annoyed with them both.

"Come on, kiddo." Alex unlocked the passenger side of her four-wheel drive and hoisted Cassie onto the seat.

At the restaurant, while Cassie used her french fries to write letters in ketchup on her plate and Alex talked about her team, Sue barely listened and eyed her daughter with growing irritation. "Quit playing with your food and eat it."

"I'm not hungry." Cassie's face glowed hotly.

Sue placed a hand on her face and felt the heat emanating from Cassie's forehead and cheeks. "I think we should go, Alex. Get some medicine in her."

Before sleep overtook them that night, Alex asked, "What were you mad about?"

"Nothing," Sue replied drowsily. "I wasn't really mad."

"What was it then?" She pushed Sue's heavy hair

away from her face as she curled herself around her back.

"It was silly."

Before daylight outlined the window, Cassie climbed into bed with her mother and Alex. "Mama, I don't feel good."

She pulled the child to her. "She's feverish, Alex."

"You better stay home, Sue," Alex said when Cassie's temperature registered one hundred and one.

"I can't today. There's a student I just have to see, the one who was hospitalized the other day. Think it's too early to call Mom?"

"It's only five. Wait an hour," Alex advised.

By ten a.m. Sue had talked to the student who had attempted suicide and made an appointment for her with a counselor at the crisis center. She was feeling good about getting that burden off her shoulders when her mother called to tell her Cassie's temperature had risen to one hundred and three.

"I hurt, Mama," Cassie complained in an uncharacteristic whine as soon as she saw her mother.

"I know, sweetie. We'll take care of that. We're going to the doctor."

When Alex returned that evening, she sat on Cassie's bed for a few minutes. "I hear you had a bad day, kiddo."

Clutching the sheet to her chin with one hand, Cassie nodded. Her thumb, which she had given up over the weekend when her father told her she was too old to suck it, was in her mouth.

"Well, you just take it easy for a few days. Okay?"

"Can I still be bat girl?" Cassie talked around the thumb.

"Of course." Hiding her concern, she smiled at the girl and smoothed the rumpled head of hair.

In the kitchen, Alex hovered behind Sue, who was fixing dinner. She rested her hands on Sue's hips and kissed her on a cheek flushed from the warmth of the stove. "She'll be all right," she said, as if wanting to hear those words from Sue.

"She will be all right, Alex."

"But you said pneumonia."

"Just the beginning. Keep her inside, give her medication. In a week she should be okay," Sue said with more assurance than she felt. "I'll have to call Ted, though."

On the morning drive to school Alex often put the finishing touches to her day's plans. Not that the day always went the way she thought it should, but at least she felt she had tried to steer it in a certain direction. Her hair fluttered in the warm breeze coming through the open truck window and she ran her fingers through her curls.

Deep in thought, she recognized Billy James only after she passed his Ford truck, hood up, parked on the shoulder of the road. Slamming on the brakes, she bounced onto the gravel berm and backed toward the pickup. The tall, lanky youth bent over the engine, the ends of his long hair dangling on the air cleaner. As she put her truck in neutral, jerked on the emergency brake, and stepped out into the warm morning, Alex heard his steady stream of curses.

"Goddamn son of a fucking bitch," he said in a low voice. "Can't afford the goddamn parts to fix it right. Have to get everything at the fucking junkyard."

Alex wondered briefly why boys wanted long hair. She always thought one of the nice things about being a male was not having to mess with one's hair.

"Hi, Miss Sundstrum." A girl she hadn't noticed opened the passenger door of the Ford and stepped onto the grassy edge of the shoulder.

"Hi, Michelle. Something wrong?" Alex approached the truck.

Billy pulled his head out from under the hood. His face turned red and he gave her a sheepish smile. "Hi. Maybe you can take Missy to school, ma'am. I got to fix this pile of junk."

"No problem. Can I give you a ride, too?" Alex stopped near the front bumper of the pickup and looked at the engine. It was astonishingly clean. "How old is this truck?" she asked Billy.

"Fifteen years," he said with an engaging grin. "Don't look it, does it?"

Shaking her head, she returned the grin. "It's nearly as old as you." The sun made her feel lethargic. She wouldn't mind spending the day basking in its warmth, she thought longingly.

"Close. My dad bought it on my third birthday." He turned his attention to the motor and buried his hands in it. "I got a generator from the junkyard last week and I think it's no good."

"Want to ride with us?" she offered again.

"No thanks. I can't leave this here."

"Are you coming to school at all?" Alex inquired.

Again Billy pulled his head out from under the hood and gave her a troubled look. "If I get this running soon, I will."

"That truck means more to him than anything," Michelle said as Alex shifted into first.

"He likes things mechanical, doesn't he?"

"He likes to work with his hands. He'd rather build a fence than watch TV."

Glancing at the girl next to her, Alex smiled. "And what do you like to do?"

"I like playing softball." Michelle played shortstop on Alex's team.

Alex doubted she would ever start and briefly wondered why she even wanted to play, because she was no more than mediocre. She looked with new curiosity at the girl, noticing how small she was, how delicate her features, and how her wild bushy blondish hair made her look like something frightened.

"I know I'm not very good, but it's fun."

"That's the whole idea," Alex remarked, pleased.

"You make it fun," the girl said in a soft voice.

Surprised, Alex smiled at her. "Thanks. You just made my day."

"It's true," Michelle continued in the same quiet tone. "All the kids think that."

Almost embarrassed, Alex kept her eyes on the road and changed the subject. "Do you usually ride to school with Billy?"

"I live just down the road from him. We're just friends. I've known him forever. He's like a brother or something."

"That's nice," Alex said, feeling an unexpected warmth toward the girl.

Before classes started Alex went to the office and told Mr. Davidson that Billy James's truck had broken down.

"Did you tell him that wouldn't excuse him from school?" Davidson asked her. He was a dapper man, neat and slender, in his late thirties, a few years older than Alex.

"No, I didn't. I knew he wouldn't leave the truck there on the road."

"He's missed enough school to be suspended already." Davidson stood, head cocked, with hands in his suit pockets and legs slightly spread.

This policy of suspending students who missed a lot of school had always troubled Alex; it punished a student's truancy by enforcing it. "I know." Alex shrugged and spread her hands, palms up. "I probably should have told him, but he looked like he had enough trouble. What about the classes he wants to take? Did you have time to look into that?"

"I'm going to find out more today. West High School offers vocational courses, but he would still have to take some academic courses here."

"What vocational courses?" she asked.

"Construction and welding and auto repair."

Excited for Billy, Alex said, "Don't suspend him without offering those choices. I'll help him with the academic stuff if I have to."

"Don't bite off more than you can chew, Alex. The kid has been in serious trouble."

"What trouble?" she asked. They stood just inside his office door. She cast a look at the clock; in five minutes the bell would ring.

34

He closed the door and walked behind his desk. "He's been into drugs. He's been drunk on the school grounds. He ran around with a bunch of kids who were really bad news."

"I know he used to run around with some pretty tough guys, but I don't think he does anymore. Didn't they get expelled last fall?"

Davidson nodded, his eyes steady on her. "I'll give him all the rope I can, Alex." He paused. "How are you doing?"

Glancing at the clock, she heard the bell ring. "Okay," she said, not wanting to think about the letter. "I've got to go. The kids'll be running my class."

Hurrying down the empty halls, she reached her classroom a little breathless. Setting her briefcase on the desk, she quieted the kids who took their seats when she appeared. The rhythm of her heart slowed to a steady beat, and she surveyed the room with a confident smile. "So, how are the projects coming?" she asked.

Several hands shot up and waved at her, begging for her attention. She called on one and turned to pick up chalk in case she wanted to emphasize a remark by putting it on the board. But she didn't glance at the board until someone made a point worth noting. Then she turned and read: *Sundstrum is a dyke.*

With the eraser in her left hand, she stared at the words, a small white scrawl, and her body reacted dramatically: her face burned, her ears rang with the pounding of her heart, her breathing quickened and shortened as if she had been punched in the stomach. Trance-like, she wiped the words from the board, wishing she could rub them out of her mind where she thought they would always be engraved. Her entire perspective had changed when she turned back toward the class.

The day crept by in a slow-moving blur. When she looked at her students, she felt only hatred. It was an exhausting and alien feeling, and she was at a loss to deal with it. Her only way to get through the class hours was to pretend nothing had happened. At noon she called home to ask about Cassie.

Sue was getting ready to leave for school. "She's better. I'm just about to go out the door. What's wrong? You sound down."

"I am." She told Sue in a low voice about the sentence on the board.

"Damn them," Sue exclaimed. She would have gladly throttled whoever wrote that message. To face the class — knowing the students had surely read the words, even if they hadn't written them — took a special kind of courage. But then Alex hadn't had a choice, had she?

"I've been in a daze all day. I can't think. I can't remember what I said from one minute to the next."

"Are you going to be all right?"

Alex knew the lack of emotion in her voice worried Sue. "Just this morning one of my players said I made softball fun. She said all the kids think that."

"Remember that, Alex. It was probably just one person who wrote that stuff on the board."

"But why didn't someone erase it before I got

there then?" Alex pressed her fingers against her eyes. Her head pounded from a massive headache.

"I don't know. Maybe the others didn't notice it. Who knows?" Sue was casting around for an explanation. What she suggested was at least possible.

"Well, I know you have to go. Give Cassie a hug for me."

At practice the girls were different. They jumped at everything Alex said and rushed to comply with her instructions. No back talk, not even the usual banter. Just the quickness to please her. Was this their way of apology or were they apprehensive of her now?

While Ben Gray worked with the pitchers and catchers, Alex noticed Billy slouched in the stands apparently waiting for Michelle. She called him down. "How about some help?"

"What?" he asked, studying his feet, scraping the dirt with one toe, reminding her of Cassie at her shyest.

"Can you throw a ball?"

" 'Course I can. I can hit one, too."

Michelle, who was swinging a bat nearby, vouched for him. "He can. He helps me."

"Well, good. You can throw to the kids with me. You know how we do that?"

"I seen you do it," he said, giving her a sharp look. With long hair tied back in a ponytail and acne-damaged skin, there was nothing particularly appealing about him.

His throw, accurate and long, was much stronger

than hers. Surprised and pleased, she watched him out of the corner of her eye. As he threw, his self-consciousness seemed to fade away and he called encouragement to the girls as they caught or missed the ball.

"Way to go, Ginger," or "Move them pegs, Missy. This ain't no golf game," or "Judge the ball. That's the way. You got a feel for it."

He might be a real asset, Alex realized, and here she had just meant to involve him in a sport to keep him out of trouble.

Before he left he gave Alex a smile which transformed him from a rather dangerous-looking young man into a beguiling boy.

Startled, Alex said, "You should smile more often, Billy."

The smile vanished in obvious embarrassment and he stalked to his truck with Michelle taking two steps to his one to keep up.

"You'd make a good coach," she said before they were out of earshot.

"Get a life," he snarled.

IV

Sue turned on Friday's early-morning news before she made coffee and was astonished when Brenda came into focus on the screen. Disheveled and wild-eyed, she stood with one of the station's regular reporters as a fireman hosed smoldering ruins in the background.

"Alex, hurry," Sue called and both Alex and Cassie responded to the urgency in her voice.

"Do you have any idea what caused the fire?" the reporter inquired.

Brenda waved her arms and her voice quavered.

"No. All of a sudden everything was in flames — my house, my garage. Thank God the barn didn't catch."

"Holy cow," Alex breathed.

Walking backward to answer the knock at the door, Sue greeted her mother without taking her eyes off the TV set.

"What's going on?" Joanne Broderick inquired.

"It's Brenda on TV, Grandma," Cassie said in a loud voice.

The reporter faced the camera and concluded, "That was Brenda Jackson, the owner of Maple Leaf Stables. The old farmhouse she called home is ashes. Firemen have not determined the cause of the three-alarm blaze."

"Poor woman," Joanne said, squeezing Cassie. "You two just go ahead. Cassie and I'll take care of things here.

Sue started toward the bedroom. "Come on, Alex, we better go to her, don't you think?"

"Look for Tabby," Cassie begged with a worried frown.

"We will, sweetie."

Sue followed Alex's little truck to the junction of Maple Leaf Drive and Smith Road. The road to Brenda's stable was blocked with official cars. Three fire engines, lights flashing, could be seen near the barn. Unable to get any closer, the women were forced to forego their plans. They agreed to meet at Brenda's after school around four-thirty.

Looking for Brenda in the barn that afternoon was like searching through a cavernous tomb. The horses were gone. Sue and Alex found their friend at the back door of the stable. Brenda's hair and face were sooty, the whites of her pale blue eyes bloodshot, her jeans and shirt dirty and rumpled.

"Brenda, where are the horses?"

Brenda stared at Sue. "I turned them all out," she said slowly.

"Oh, Brenda, I'm so sorry. We were here early today, just after we saw you on the tube, but we couldn't get through." She wanted to comfort Brenda and reached for her.

"You're too clean," Brenda protested, backing away.

"We tried to call you all day," Alex explained.

Cats appeared and wound themselves around Brenda's legs, purring. Sue spotted Tabby, tail high and back arched, rubbing against her leg with three others. They sounded like small revved-up motors.

Brenda suddenly sat on the door stoop and covered her face with her hands. "They're hungry. I should feed them. I should bring in some horses. But I can't seem to do anything."

Alex said, "Tell us what to do and we'll do it, Brenda. Then come home with us and stay tonight."

"No, I can't leave. It might happen again," Brenda protested, raising her voice in alarm.

Alex soothed her. "Okay, okay. Let's do what has to be done, though."

They spent the next couple hours helping Brenda round up the horses and feed them, eventually accepting her wish to stay at the barn that night.

Cassie and her grandmother were removing a casserole from the oven when Alex and Sue finally arrived home. "Sorry, Mom," Sue said. "We had to go to Brenda's and help her."

"It's okay. Cassie and I fixed dinner while we were waiting." The older woman rested a hand on her granddaughter's head and smiled at her. "She's a good little cook. But now I have to run." Joanne removed Sue's apron. "How is Brenda?"

"She'll be okay. The place needs cleaning up, though." Alex thought again how much Sue resembled her mother, their hair and eyes and figures similar in color and shape. "Why don't you stay and eat with us, Joanne? You fixed it," she said.

"I'd love to, but Mike and I are eating with friends tonight."

"Mom, can you take Cassie tomorrow? We need to help Brenda."

"I wish I could but your dad and I are going north with the same friends. It's been in the works for a long time." She hugged Cassie and then her daughter.

"I want to go to Brenda's too," Cassie said, looking stubborn.

Alex answered the phone as Sue showed her mother out the door. "It's Ted," she said, handing Sue the receiver, annoyed because he refused to acknowledge her.

Alex heard the hesitation in Sue's voice. "Change weekends? Cassie can't go outside, you know."

Seldom did Ted's plans fit theirs so well, Alex thought. She glanced at Cassie, who was carrying silverware to the table. Her hair waved softly to her shoulders, wisps of it framing her red cheeks; her eyes were large and luminous; she looked angelic in a toe-length nightgown.

"Okay, sure. Just give us an hour or two to eat dinner and get ready." Sue hung up and said, "Pack your bag, Cassie. Your dad will be here after dinner."

Cassie threw the silverware she had been clutching onto the table, where it skittered across the surface and fell to the floor. Screaming, "I don't wanna go," she ran down the hall to her room.

"Goodness," Alex commented as Sue marched after her daughter.

"What's the matter with you, young lady?" Sue asked, and Alex knew Sue was hearing echoes of her mother's voice from her own youth. Words she had once sworn she would never say to her child. She stood, hands on hips, next to the bed where the little girl had thrown herself face down.

"I wanna go to the barn," Cassie wailed.

"Well, you can't go outside until the doctor says you can. I've half a mind to wallop you."

Alex came silently to Sue and placed a hand on her back but said nothing.

"I'll tell Daddy," Cassie threatened between sobs.

"Tell him you don't want to spend the weekend with him," Sue remarked, going to the closet and removing the small suitcase. She opened Cassie's dresser drawers and tossed some underwear into the overnight bag.

Cassie sat up and snatched the underwear her mother had just put into the suitcase and threw it toward the dresser. Alex watched this tableau with astonishment and an unwelcome touch of amusement.

Sue turned from the dresser and was met with

the thrown panties. She and Cassie stared at each other. Cassie perched on her knees, tears spilling down her cheeks, her lower lip jutting. Alex guessed Cassie was as amazed by her own actions as Alex and Sue were.

Then Sue laughed and collapsed on the bed. She held her midsection and rolled with laughter, grabbing Cassie on one of the rolls. "Cassandra Sue, you're a brat," she said. "What makes you think you can get away with stuff like this?"

Cassie wrapped her arms around her mother's neck and small peals of laughter erupted from her. "Do I have to go, Mama?" she asked after Sue stopped laughing and lay still, holding her daughter.

"You do."

"Well, how about dinner?" Alex asked, looking at them with a grin of relief.

After Cassie left with her father, Alex asked Sue about the scene in the bedroom. "I never saw Cassie so disobedient."

"You never saw Cassie so thwarted."

"Reminded me of you." Alex crossed her arms and studied Sue. "Should you have laughed?"

"I couldn't help it. Suddenly it just seemed funny — me packing her stuff and her throwing it out of the suitcase. Of course, it wasn't really funny, was it?"

"It was funny, but it won't be when she's thirteen."

"Yeah," Sue agreed and then said with a touch of irony, "I can't wait."

"Neither can I."

* * * * *

44

"Doesn't spring feel good?" Alex asked as she turned her truck into the driveway leading to Brenda's barn. The vehicle bounced in the ruts and threw dust into the air behind it.

Spitting pieces of hair out of her mouth, Sue held the rest of it in a thick ponytail behind her head, wrapping a band around it. "Maybe I'll get my hair cut short for summer."

"Please don't."

"Yours is short," Sue pointed out.

"I love your hair."

"It's so heavy when it's hot," Sue complained, but she knew she wouldn't go against Alex's wishes.

The ash, still wet and thick and warm, sucked at their boots and coated their clothes as they picked through it, where the house had once stood. Why were they doing this? Sue wanted to ask. What could be worth saving if it had been in this muck? Who would want it?

Just then Alex pulled a metal box out of the ash; it came loose with a slurping sound. "Look, Brenda," she called, and both Brenda and Sue turned toward her.

"Great. Those are my boarding records." Brenda tried to move and fell forward, burying her hands up to her elbows in the ash. "Goddamn it all to hell," she said, pulling herself upright and shaking globs of muck off herself.

Alex and Sue laughed.

"It's like walking in cow shit or something," Brenda said with a sheepish grin as she lifted one foot and then the other in an awkward, exaggerated high-stepping walk.

"What do you think you're doing?"

Their heads swung toward the source of the strange male voice. Two men in what looked like waders were standing at the edge of the rubble.

"Looking for something worth saving," Brenda replied. "What the hell do you think we're doing, and who are you?"

"We're from the arson squad, lady. You just might screw up any clues as to how this fire started. Didn't anyone tell you not to touch anything?"

"Oh," Brenda said, suddenly deflated. "No, at least I don't remember anyone saying anything like that."

"Well, come on out of the muck and let us get to work. What we find, we'll set aside for you."

The three women, moving in slow motion, extricated themselves from the rubble.

"So much for that," Brenda said.

"What can we do now?" Sue asked.

"Help me in the barn. I'm moving into the lounge till I can get a house trailer." Brenda half-heartedly brushed the drying sludge from her arms and clothes, then started toward the barn.

"Why are you looking at me like that?" Sue asked as she and Alex followed in Brenda's wake. She knew she was dirty, that her hair was tangled and her clothes a mess.

"Mmm," Alex said, as if wanting very much to throw her in the mud and ravish her. Laughing, she shook her head.

"Piggy," Sue muttered, returning the crooked grin.

"How did you guess?"

"I know that look."

They washed in the bathroom adjacent to the lounge, where a toilet, sink, and rusty shower stall were crammed into the small space. The lounge was furnished with a cracked vinyl recliner and couch, an old kitchen table with four straight chairs, an ancient stained refrigerator and stove. Dust and cobwebs were everywhere, and Sue attacked them with a broom and rag, knowing she was wasting her time, that they would start returning before she finished brushing them away.

Alex helped Brenda in the barn, filling water buckets and cleaning stalls. The barn girl, Tracey, silently worked with them.

"Did you have any insurance?" Alex asked Brenda as the two of them turned out a couple horses.

"Some, maybe enough to buy a trailer and a used truck and build a garage. My truck was in the garage when it burned." They paused to watch the horses thud off, sending clods of earth flying from their hooves. Dust motes danced in the sunlight filtering through the open barn door. Sparrows fought nearby over grain in a pile of manure.

When Alex and Brenda entered the lounge, they were greeted with smells of chicken and rice baking. Sue had driven to the store and bought groceries and staples for Brenda, stocked the refrigerator and shelves next to it with her purchases, and begun dinner.

"It never smelled like this in here before. This is great, Sue," Brenda said. "You didn't by any chance buy any liquor? I'd kill for a drink."

"Thought you might. Look in the freezer."

Brenda whooped as she brought out a bottle of vodka. "I'll do the honors. What's there to mix this with?"

"Look in the fridge," Sue said, putting a salad together.

Alex came up behind Sue and wrapped her arms around her. "You sweetie," she said.

"Careful," Sue admonished, looking around.

"It's just us three. Right, Brenda?"

"Tracey went home. The horses are eating. We should be alone."

"In that case," Sue said, turning and putting her arms around Alex. "Phew, you smell like a horse."

Alex grinned and shrugged. "That's what it's like when you work and eat with the animals. What can I say?"

Handing them each a drink, Brenda opened the door to the cats who had been waiting just outside. The three women sat at the table and toasted Brenda's safety, the horses' survival, the cats' many lives, a new beginning for Brenda. They ate everything Sue put on the table.

"I wondered what happened to that look in your eye," Sue said as Alex drew her close.

"We're home, we're clean, we're in bed, and I could just fall asleep," Alex murmured.

Sue nibbled at the slender neck, then kissed the freckles on Alex's shoulders. She caressed the slim, long, firm body, enjoying the feel of silky warm skin. Slipping a hand between Alex's legs, she gently inched her way into the warm wet inner reaches.

"How about a quickie? Think you can stay awake long enough?"

"I'll give it a try," Alex said, breathing faster at the touch. She covered Sue's mouth with her own and slid a hand under Sue's arm and into her crotch.

Daylight showed around the blinds as Sue dragged herself onto an elbow, reaching to silence the ringing phone. She listened so long that Alex, who was also wakened from a deep sleep, said, "What is it?"

Sue waved her arm for quiet and whispered, "It's Brenda." Then said into the receiver, "We're coming. Just hang in there."

"Now what?" Alex asked, falling back on her pillow.

"It was arson, not even a well-concealed case of arson," Sue said quietly.

Brenda was in the barn with a revolver strapped to her hip when they arrived. Sue, who didn't believe the general public should have access to guns and certainly not when children were around, took one horrified look and nearly laughed. With boots and jeans and a gun, Brenda looked like a character out of a bad western. "All you need is a hat," she remarked dryly.

"Well, I've got to protect myself. I have to protect the horses."

"Most people end up shooting someone by accident when they've got a gun and are jumpy," Sue said. Alex looked at Sue, who explained, "I read it in the paper."

"If somebody burned your place down, you'd carry a gun too." Brenda defended herself, then added,

"There are these boys hanging around. I saw them in that abandoned gas station on the corner."

"Maybe they're fascinated with fire," Sue suggested.

They headed outside, blinking from the already bright sunlight. Billy James was slouched on the bench with two other tough-looking young men. "Billy, what are you doing here?" Alex asked, startled.

"Ms. Sundstrum, ma'am." He jumped to his feet, looking alarmed. "What are you doin' here?"

"I asked first."

He shrugged, the deadpan expression she thought he must strive to achieve back in place. It aged him. "Lookin' for work."

"Work? Are you looking for help?" Alex turned to Brenda, who lifted her shoulders noncommittally.

The other two boys appeared even more menacing than Billy with their arms crossed, sleeves rolled up over stringy biceps, cigarettes dangling from thin lips, their narrowed eyes following the conversation. While she couldn't have said exactly what it was about these young men that frightened her, they exuded an aura of danger.

"Thought maybe you might want someone to do some building. Me and my friends could build a garage," he said. "If you're interested, call me." He wrote his name and number on a dirty piece of paper and thrust it at Brenda. "I live not far from here, you know, on Smith Road."

"I'll think about it," Brenda said.

"See ya," Billy said over his shoulder as he

swaggered to a rusting Monte Carlo with his two disreputable-looking companions. They left in a black cloud of exhaust.

"That's Billy James, that hoody-looking kid? I wouldn't trust him out of sight," Sue remarked.

"They all look like bad news to me."

"He's not so bad in the right surroundings."

On Monday the doctor told Sue that Cassie could resume outside activities with normal caution.

At the softball game Tuesday Cassie rushed to the dugout and nearly ran into Billy, who had just lugged out the game equipment and dumped it near the fence.

Alex introduced the two. "Billy's our new manager," she explained.

"I am not," he protested.

"You said if you're here, you'll help. Right? Same thing." Alex looked in the stands toward Sue and smiled faintly, then noticed Mrs. Westover the next seat down.

After winning their first game, which had been non-conference, Alex's players had lost the next two rather badly. She wanted softball to be fun, but she didn't relish the thought of being rock-bottom in the standings. She turned her attention to her players. "Okay girls, go get 'em. Do it this time."

"Hear that?" Billy shouted after the starters as they ran to their field positions. "Don't drag tail."

Cassie stopped lining up bats and stared at him.

"What do you think, squirt?" he said with a grin and a pat on her back. "Need to get the lead out, don't they? Need to hit some wood."

Alex flinched a little at his words. She stood nearby, hands in her back pockets. Ben, with one foot high in the fence behind home plate, glanced at her. Alex knew her decision to ask Billy to manage was not a popular one. The parents, the faculty, even the girls looked at him suspiciously. He wasn't exactly the All-American Boy.

The team squeaked a loser. One run behind, the fifth batter up struck out in the bottom of the seventh, leaving two on base.

Billy helped Cassie gather equipment to return to the storage shed. "Next time, huh, squirt?" he said, bending his long skinny frame to gather up balls.

Cassie nodded shyly.

After the game, Alex noticed Mrs. Westover standing with Lisa Gavinski and started toward them as soon as she could free herself from parents and kids. Nancy Westover grunted in answer to Alex's compliment, "Kelly pitched well." She had put Kelly in at the top of the fifth, apparently not soon enough to suit her mother, Alex gathered.

"How'd your team do?" Alex asked Lisa. The junior varsity girls played their games at a nearby diamond at the same time as the varsity.

"Good. It was called after the fifth."

Envy held Alex in its grip. "Congratulations. You saw some of ours then?"

"I watched the last inning with Mrs. Westover here." A smile caused Lisa's lips to twitch. "Bad luck."

"Oh, I don't think it's that. They just can't seem

to hit the ball. I wanted to tell you Kelly will start next game," Alex said to Kelly's mother, who stared resolutely at a spot between Alex and Lisa. Alex followed her gaze, which was fixed on Sue and Cassie, who stood near the bleachers.

"Maybe they'll win then," Mrs. Westover said rudely and walked to her car.

"She won reelection, you know," Lisa remarked as they watched the short, stout woman slide behind the wheel of her dark green older-model El Dorado.

"Aren't we lucky?" Alex said dryly. Lisa was referring to the school board election. She suddenly realized that Mrs. Westover would have received a copy of the letter, too. It gave her an unpleasant start.

V

More than half of Sue's work day was spent
helping students plan their schedules to fit with
future plans or present actualities. The remainder
went to students with problems, such as Tammy
Faye, the girl who'd attempted suicide, who sat
across from her desk now, and whom Sue had sent
to counseling more than a month ago.

"Perhaps if you moved out of the house," Sue
suggested as she had before. "Can you live with a
friend or relative, Tammy?" The abusive father
seemed to be the stumbling block — and a mother

who either feared him too much to ask him to leave or feared being alone more than being abused.

"I can't," the girl said as she had before, her young-old face small and pinched.

"Why not?"

"Well, I thought maybe if I just kept my mouth shut it would be all right."

Sue had a difficult time with abusive parents. It was so hard to convince their children that no matter what they did they wouldn't please such a parent. "You're still going to the crisis center, right?"

The girl nodded solemnly. "He don't want me to, though."

"Promise you'll talk to me before you stop counseling," Sue said, leaning forward.

When Tammy left, she called Ted and was put through to him by his secretary. "Ted, I don't like the things I'm hearing from Cassie," she said without preamble.

"Let's meet for lunch," he replied. "I'm going to be near the school."

When she arrived at the restaurant down the street from Chancelor High, Ted was already seated. Always a surface gentleman, she thought as he stood when she slid into the booth.

Just over six feet tall, his body was hard and fit. People were always commenting on how much Cassie looked like him, because of the dark wavy hair and hazel eyes. Smiling faintly, he met Sue's gaze. "You look good."

"Thanks. I hear you have a girlfriend," she said.

"Is that the problem?" He raised thick eyebrows in question.

"No, of course not." She stirred sugar and milk

into her coffee and looked around to see who was within earshot. Her colleagues often lunched here. "Cassie says you're buying a house and want her to live with you during the week." She harbored a desperate hope that he would tell her this was not so.

"That's right. I can give her a healthy environment, the kind a kid needs."

"The agreement was that she live with me during the week and spend every other weekend and alternate holidays with you," Sue reminded him in low, angry tones.

"I'm challenging the agreement," he replied calmly. "You'll be getting notice."

Sue felt as if a fist had closed tightly around her heart, the beat pausing and picking up speed. "Stop telling her how I live is wrong."

"The way you live is wrong," he said with complete self-possession, picking up his sandwich. "I don't want her exposed to that so much of the time. I want her to have a positive role model."

Sue had no appetite. She stared at her food as her eyes filled with tears. "Don't do this, Ted," she whispered in a choked voice.

"It's for her own good," he said self-righteously.

"I won't just let her go." Sue half-rose off the seat.

"I didn't expect you to."

"I love her. She likes living with us." Sue grabbed her purse and slung it over her shoulder.

"I love her, too." He stood when she did. "Aren't you going to eat?"

"I'm not hungry."

His eyes wandered over her. "Suit yourself."

She made her way back to school. Putting her head on her desk, she sobbed until she was forced to put away her own grief and fears to counsel others.

Before Alex left for the airport Saturday to pick up her parents, Sue and Cassie went to the barn. It was a busy place, and after Cassie rode, Sue chatted with Brenda for a while. Cassie stood near the garage Billy James was building and watched him hammer two-by-sixes to hold up trusses.

Sue and Alex had been surprised that Brenda hired the boy for the job, but Brenda had explained that he was willing to do the work for very little money. "He said he wanted the experience," she had told Alex and Sue.

"Whatcha doin', squirt?" Billy called down from his ladder. "I seen you ride. How do you stay on?"

"Brenda says it's a balancing act," Cassie said solemnly. "How come you're doing that?"

"For money, honey. How come you ride?"

The sun gently warmed them. A soft breeze carried odors of blooming plants with it. "It's fun." She held up Tabby for him to see. "My cat lives here."

"I got one dog and so many cats I can't count them."

"Brenda has that many cats. Daddy says I can have a dog if I live with him during the week."

Sue and Brenda walked over. Sue called a hello to Billy.

"Hello, Ms. Carruthers." Then to Brenda, "How'm I doing?"

"Just great. I never saw anything go up so fast."

"What happened to the two guys who were hanging around with him after the fire?" Sue asked Brenda in a soft voice.

She shrugged. "I don't know. He's the only one working for me." Already tan, Brenda looked relaxed and healthy, her jitters over the fire apparently gone. There was no revolver at her hip.

"When's the house trailer coming?"

"As soon as they finish clearing the site for it." She pointed at the bulldozer parked on the house ruins.

Alex arrived at the airport an hour before her parents' flight was due because her brother, David, wanted to talk to her.

Alex's parents had retired to Merritt Island in Florida two winters ago. They returned for visits spring, summer and fall, usually two weeks at a time, and divided their stay between Alex and David. David was also unmarried and three years older than his sister. Alex suspected her brother was single for the same reason she was. He lived a few miles west of Chancelor and taught journalism at the local university extension and was a contributing editor and writer for a regional magazine.

David, tall and thin, waited in the small airport's restaurant. He smiled at his sister. He was a male replica of her. He mirrored her eyes and hair and frame, except his was masculine. Sitting across from him, she grinned in greeting. They saw little of each other, considering the miles between them were few.

"So, how are you?" she asked.

"Want some coffee?"

"Decaffeinated."

"Am I wrong about us?" he began, eyebrows lifted in question. His expressive face interested her. She wondered if hers showed so much emotion.

"What do you mean?" she asked warily.

"I live with a man, you live with a woman," he said with a shrug, his mouth twisting.

Serious situations always made her want to laugh and she did. "Surprise, surprise," she said.

He held up a hand. "That's not the problem. Remember I told you I was writing a book?" She nodded. "Well, it's being published."

"That's great, David. I am so proud of you." She studied his face. "Your book is a little revealing? Is that it? You're worried about Mom and Dad?"

"More worried about Dad," he said with a wry smile, hunched over his coffee cup.

Alex was inordinately fond of her father. He had wanted his son to be an athlete, but David had spurned organized sports. Alex, by contrast, excelled at them. Her dad had made light of his son's accomplishments by focusing almost exclusively on his daughter's. Gradually, the rift between father and son had extended to brother and sister. "You gotta do what you gotta do," she said. "You can't live your life for someone else. You know? You really can't."

"I know that. I'm not ready to tell them about it, though. I'd just as soon keep it quiet."

"If that's what you want, David, but what a shame. Mom would be so pleased."

"Until she read it."

They watched the plane taxi to the terminal and the passengers offload down the portable steps, making their way to the building. From this distance her parents appeared younger than they were — her dad pencil-straight with thick white hair, her mother nearly as tall as her father, slender and dignified-looking.

"Look at you two, so handsome. Do you understand why they haven't been taken, Bud?" Maryanne Sundstrum asked her husband as the four of them stood by baggage pick-up waiting for suitcases to appear on the carousel.

"Maybe they don't want to be," Bud grunted.

David raised his eyebrows to Alex as if to say I told you so, and Alex laughed.

"What's funny, dear?" her mother inquired.

"Nothing, Mom." She wanted desperately to tell her mother that she was taken and so was her brother.

They left David in the parking lot, agreeing to meet at Alex's apartment the next day.

Whenever Alex's parents visited, they slept in Alex and Sue's bed and the two younger women moved in with Cassie, taking the twin beds and putting her on a cot. In the past Cassie had spent most of their visits with her father, but this was her weekend with her mother and Sue, feeling she had already lost her, was unwilling to let her go.

Alex worked on dinner with her mother while her dad watched the television news. After Sue and Cassie came home, amid the exchange of greetings, Cassie rushed down the hall to her room and brought out her latest papers to show Maryanne and Bud. He lifted her on his knee.

It looked to Alex, who had been somewhat worried about what Cassie might say, as if the visit would go well. She and Sue went to the kitchen to finish the dinner preparations.

Alex could hear most of the conversation between her parents and Cassie as, all pretense of shyness gone, Cassie regaled them with accounts of the fire and school and her experiences as bat girl.

"How did it go with David?" Sue asked as she put rolls in the oven.

"I'll tell you later. He'll be over tomorrow for dinner around seven."

David did not come alone. He brought John Donaldson with him and introduced him to his parents as his roommate. John was short and muscular. His gray eyes laughed when he did and his smile revealed long white teeth with gaps between them.

Cassie carried them through dinner. Sue uncharacteristically allowed her to babble to fill the awkward silences. There was a marked difference of opinion between the generations and on certain topics everyone treaded carefully, avoiding politics, religion and lifestyles.

Watching her mother, Alex thought she could see the older woman thinking how nice it would be if Sue paired off with David and she did the same with John. Alex whispered as much in Sue's ear as they cleaned up after dinner.

"Well, he is cute. He looks like you," Sue commented.

"Who's cute?" David asked from just behind them. He ate a carrot from the nearly empty hors d'oeuvres plate and leaned against the counter, crossing his ankles. "Nice little girl," he said to Sue. "Just what Mom and Dad would like us to produce, which of course we won't."

"Well, maybe she can substitute," Sue suggested.

"How did you ever hook up with someone so interested in sports?" Alex asked, handing him a dish towel.

David retorted, "He's not all that interested. You have to talk about something with Dad, and John's good at chit-chat. Sue, Alex was number one jock in our family, the apple of Daddy's eye." His smile belied his words and the edge in his voice.

"It was a topsy-turvy family. Don't hold it against me anymore, David," Alex said.

"I'll work on it," he promised.

The following week strained the fabric of the small family Alex and Sue and Cassie had formed. The addition of two adults to the household in itself would have been difficult to assimilate, but because they were Alex's parents, and ignorant of Sue and Alex's relationship, life became an act and conversations were often artificial and awkward. Only Cassie seemed unaware of any tension, relishing the attention Alex's parents bestowed on her.

On Thursday, Sue received official notice of Ted's intentions toward Cassie. Mail in hand, she beat a retreat to Cassie's room and closed the door quietly behind her, leaving Cassie to entertain Bud, and Alex and Maryanne to prepare the meal. Sue sat on the edge of the bed, knowing that the painful emptiness would stay with her when primary custody of Cassie was awarded to Ted. There was no doubt in her mind that she would lose. It was just a matter of when.

When Alex pushed open the door to Cassie's room, Sue was still slouched on one of the beds, the court paper dangling from her hand. "What is it, babe?" she asked, softly shutting the door behind her.

Sue handed her the paper, and Alex sank onto the bed next to the woman she loved and put an arm around her. "What now?" she asked quietly.

"Now we meet with the family counselor or commissioner, whatever he or she's called, then the court decides. Maybe they'll appoint a guardian to represent Cassie." She shrugged. "It doesn't matter. She's as good as gone."

Alex hugged her closer but said nothing. She was thinking about weeks without Cassie and hoping the child wouldn't be removed completely from Sue's custody.

"I'll be all right, Alex. You go on out with your parents before they begin to wonder what's going on."

When Alex's parents left for her brother's, Alex breathed a sigh of relief. "At last. I love them, but there's certainly a lot to be said for being honest. I don't think I could pretend another day that you and I are just friends."

Sue smiled. "I thought Cassie would give it all away before now."

"It's crazy, you know. My brother writes a book he thinks he can't tell our parents about. You and I pretend we're 'just friends.' It's like playing hide and seek our entire lives."

* * * * *

The last week in May Ted and Sue were scheduled to meet with the Family Court Commissioner. Somehow, Sue thought, she had to enlighten her parents about the impending events without revealing Ted's motives. She also had to discuss Cassie's future with her child, the possible change in living arrangements. Night after night, she woke sweating with anxiety, and lay quietly staring at the ceiling, sometimes until daylight. Her temper frayed from lack of sleep and nagging worry, causing her to snap at the slightest aggravation.

The lovely weather at the beginning of the month had deteriorated to cold, windy, rainy days. Watching softball, hunched in winter jacket and a blanket, wasn't her idea of after-work fun, especially with the added worry of the effects of the inclement weather on Cassie, who was so bundled her movements were restricted.

"I would rather it had been cold at the beginning of the month," Sue muttered to Kathy Gray as they drew warmth from each other in the stands the third week in May.

Ginger blew on her fingers and pitched another ball, walking the third batter in a row. Alex paced outside the fence and Billy stood shivering in a sweatshirt just behind Cassie, having wrapped her in his jacket. Hands on her shoulders, he held her against his long, skinny legs. "Come on, Ginger. Send it across the plate. You can do it," he yelled.

Sue watched them — the tall, gangling, homely boy and the small, sturdy, red-cheeked child. An unlikely pair, she thought with a smile. Who would have guessed Billy to have such a tender spot.

Looking miserable, Ginger put her hands under her armpits and then threw a strike.

"Way to go," Billy hollered.

Alex replaced Ginger with Kelly in the top of the fifth. The two girls were now alternating as starters, usually replacing each other during the latter half of a game.

Sue had noticed a change in Kelly's mother since her daughter had become a regular starter. Mrs. Westover said hello to Sue and spoke to Alex when addressed by her. As the fifth inning progressed, Kelly began to have the same difficulty pitching as Ginger had.

"It's the cold," Kathy Gray said. "Remember the last game?"

"How could I forget," Sue remarked, recalling an even colder day. She hunched further into her jacket as the game slowly progressed with both teams exchanging runs, until the bottom of the seventh when Alex's team suddenly came alive after two were out and pulled ahead by one run which brought the game to an end. None too soon for Sue, whose fingertips were numb.

Placing Cassie on his shoulders, Billy whooped around outside the dugout, slapping the winning players on their backs. Cassie clutched his ponytail, her little body jerking to his victory dance.

The girls had accepted Billy after a few practices when he had proved to be apt at softball. While Ben worked with the pitchers and catchers, Billy spent his time batting and throwing to the fielders, patiently instructing the girls to swing at the right moment to bring bat in contact with ball. Alex supervised the group like a pro, Sue thought.

Billy fit well into the sport, and Alex helped him during her free hour with his academic studies. When he applied himself to learning, she told Sue, he did well enough and she enjoyed what she considered his honest outlook on life.

"My ma she thinks I should be president of some company someday. You know?" he had said to her earlier that week. "She works cleaning offices at KCC. My dad says I'm no good, she says I could be a president. Crazy, ain't it? Me, all I want to do is make a living."

"Brenda's garage is coming along nicely. You do good work."

"It's okay. Good experience," he had replied modestly.

"Brenda said you're doing it for fifty bucks. That's nothing. Her insurance is paying for it."

"She can use that money for something else," he had said. "She's not such a tough lady, you know."

"You're a soft touch, Billy."

He had given her an indecipherable look. "It's my head that's soft, I think."

Sue stiffly descended the bleachers to stand with Kathy Gray and Ben near Alex. Cassie, still in Billy's jacket, helped him pick up equipment and stow it in the storage shed. Instead of heading for her car, Nancy Westover stood silently nearby.

"Ginger and Kelly pitched well, considering the cold," Alex said to the parents.

Rather than grunting or turning her back, Mrs. Westover nodded.

* * * * *

Unable to put off the talk with her parents any longer, Sue called her mother from work the following day and asked to see them that evening. The whole experience saddened her. She had just seen Tammy Faye and the girl's problems with her father put Ted into Sue's mind, but only because he was Cassie's father. When she watched Ted with Cassie, she was reminded of why she had married him. He became awkward in his attempts at gentleness.

Walking up the long sidewalk to her parents' condominium was not coming home for Sue. She still missed with a pang the comfortable house in which she had grown up. Although the buildings and grounds were luxurious, Sue always felt as if she were in a public place — a motel or hotel or park. Her mother opened the door to her knock and she stepped into her parents' lives.

Her father looked up from his chair, the open newspaper in his lap, his balding head reflecting the light from the floor lamp.

Sue bent to kiss him after hugging her mother. "Haven't seen you for a while, Dad," she said with a resentment she hadn't known was there. She studied him and noticed the thin broken blood vessels around his nose and cheeks, his face florid and puffy. "You all right?"

"Getting a little fat in my retirement but otherwise having a good time." He patted the paunch he had been putting on for years.

"Sit down, honey," her mother said.

Sue took a deep breath. "Ted is going to try to

change the custody arrangement for Cassie. I thought I should tell you."

"Why is he doing that?" her mother asked.

"He's got a girlfriend; he's buying a house; he thinks he can give her a better home life than I can." Was she defending Ted's motives or trying to hide them?

"Would you still have her some of the time?" Joanne asked, her expression troubled.

A flash of insight told Sue that her mother knew about her relationship with Alex. "I'd probably have the same custody arrangement that he has now. The court date is set for the last week in May."

"I'll talk to him," Mike Broderick said suddenly. He had been a senior partner in the firm where Ted worked.

"No, don't." Panic flooded Sue with adrenalin. She was sure Ted would level with her father.

Joanne frowned slightly. "Your dad has always gotten along well with Ted."

"Why did you tell us then?" Sue's father asked abruptly.

"I thought you ought to know."

"But you won't let me try to help."

"No, Dad." And she had to wonder if keeping Cassie was less important to her than a confrontation with her parents over her sexual orientation.

In Alex's mind, the differences between BL and AL — Before the Letter and After the Letter — were difficult for her to pin down with words. They were subtle changes and sometimes, such as now, sitting in her principal's office, she wondered if they existed only in her imagination.

She had been cursorily summoned to Davidson's office and had noticed, not for the first time, that he couldn't or wouldn't meet her eyes. Then, as she sat at his bidding, she thought of other things — how her superintendent, who stood near the door, had turned down a side hall earlier in the day as if to avoid her. And it wasn't the first time that had happened, either. Sometimes faculty conversation stopped long enough for her to wonder whether she had been the topic when she entered the teachers' lounge. She even sensed a change in the students, an aloofness in some of them. Billy James hadn't abandoned her, though.

Billy had yet to miss a practice or a game, was more than halfway finished with Brenda's garage, and dutifully struggled through Alex's tutoring during her free period. But Billy was removed from the mainstream of school life. He spent his mornings at West High School and only returned in the afternoon for her tutoring and two classes.

Maybe she looked for differences, she thought, glancing from one man to the other, wondering why they wanted to see her.

"We asked you here to talk about Billy James," Davidson began.

"What about Billy?" Alex asked, startled because she had been thinking about him.

Superintendent Orbison lowered his bulk onto a chair near hers and leaned toward her. "There was a fire some weeks ago. The police have good reason to believe Billy James was involved in it."

She felt her body stiffen as the pieces clicked into place in her mind. Billy and the other two boys at the barn, Billy working on the garage for next to nothing. "Have they arrested him?" she asked quietly.

"They just want to question him now, but they can't find him. Do you know where he is?"

She shook her head wearily and pictured Cassie on Billy's shoulders. "If it's true, what a waste," she said, knowing she should be furious with him. After all, it was her friend's home and garage that had been destroyed, putting Brenda's life into jeopardy. But if the accusation were true, he had tried to make amends. Wasn't that why he was rebuilding the garage?

Alex drove Michelle home after practice. "I'm going to Billy's," she told the girl. "Will you point the way?"

"Two houses further down the road on the same side." Michelle slid out of the truck. "Thanks for the ride."

Parking next to a rusting seventies-model Chrysler perched on cement blocks in the driveway, Alex sat for a moment and looked at the old farmhouse. Its paint was badly peeled. Near the front door in tall grass stood a rusty push mower. She stepped down from the truck and started toward the front door.

From around the corner of the house came a barking ball of fury. Paralyzed by fear, Alex watched the dog throw itself at her. She turned to run at the last minute and the animal, which appeared to be part German shepherd and part Labrador retriever, latched onto her pant leg and pinched her skin. Screaming for help, she fell to the grass in her efforts to get away.

"Git off her, Pal. Go on, git."

On her hands and knees, Alex looked up at the immense woman standing on the front stoop, hollering at the dog. Pal released her leg and, tail between legs, vanished around the corner of the house. Alex struggled to her feet and wiped herself off.

The woman took a step down from the stoop. "You all right, Miss?"

Looking at her wet pant leg, Alex saw no blood. "I guess. What a fierce dog." She glanced nervously toward the direction the dog had taken.

"He won't hurt you."

Alex recovered herself enough to introduce herself and ask, "Are you Mrs. James, Billy's mother?" And when the woman nodded, she looked for glimpses of Billy in her but saw the resemblance only in the narrow gray eyes peeking out of the wary face.

"He told me about you. You done a lot for him." Then she asked in a flat voice, "What do you want with him?"

"He wasn't at school today. I need to talk to him. Do you know where he is?"

"No," she said in that curiously expressionless voice. "I'll tell him you're looking when I see him. I'll keep the dog off you while you get to your truck."

Alex took the hint. She beat a fast retreat to the

Chevy, casting furtive glances behind her to make certain the dog wasn't about to launch himself at her again.

Because of softball, they never ate before seven during the week, and it would have been much later without Sue's efforts. Normally this arrangement wouldn't have bothered Sue, but since Cassie's custody hearing was only a week away, everything bothered her. She still awakened flushed with panic at night, and she experienced moments during the day when the same anxiety overtook her. Her breathing quickened, her heart pounded, her mind refused to focus on other problems, and she had to force herself to breathe deeply and slowly until it passed.

She and Cassie had just made a tuna dish and put it in the oven when Alex arrived home. "Late as usual," Sue said, her annoyance surfacing when Alex came up behind her and kissed her on the neck.

Alex moved away, withdrawing from Sue's anger. Turning on the television, she sat down in silence. Cassie crawled up on the couch next to her.

Wiping her hands on a towel, Sue watched them and tried to quell her irritation. She lost the battle and said, "I work all day, too, you know, and then I have to fix dinner every night."

Alex stared glumly back at her, obviously not expecting Sue's outburst. "You don't have to fix anything for me. I'm not hungry."

"You mean I went to the bother to buy stuff and

make a casserole and you're not going to eat it?"
Sue heard her voice rising.

"I'll eat it, Mama. I'm hungry."

"I'll eat it too, Sue. Don't get all excited."

"Don't do me any favors." Sue felt her eyes fill with tears, and she turned away before they overflowed.

"I don't need this kind of crap," Alex said, rising to her feet and going to their room.

"I don't need this crap either." Cassie stared angrily at her mother, her small fists balled on her hips.

Sue headed down the hall after Alex with Cassie following. "Don't talk that way in front of Cassie," she said, opening the door Alex had shut behind her.

Alex, lying on the bed with hands behind her head, turned toward Sue. "Don't you talk that way in front of her then."

Appalled at her own behavior, Sue didn't know how to make things right and didn't realize she was crying until she tasted the tears.

"Hey, babe," Alex said softly. "Come here."

Cassie hesitantly joined their embrace, making it a circle.

"I'm sorry," Sue said in a choked voice.

"It's okay. We'll talk about it later," Alex soothed.

"You're crabby, Mama," Cassie said.

"I know," Sue admitted. "I'm a bear."

But once Cassie was in bed, Sue said accusingly, "You weren't any prize tonight either." They stood on the patio in the near dark, watching the sun sink slowly out of sight. A warm breeze carried the sweet smell of honeysuckle.

Alex explained what had happened that day. "I don't know whether to be furious with him or worried about his safety."

"I'm not surprised," Sue remarked thoughtfully. "It all fits, doesn't it?"

"Unfortunately, yes." Alex sighed deeply. "Doesn't it make you feel bad when one of your kids is such a disappointment?"

"I've got that girl, Tammy Faye. She's just going to repeat her parents' behavior. I see it over and over. Her dad abuses her, her mother ignores it. The kid tries to please them both; she fails in school. She'll be just like her mother in ten years, married to some guy who beats her and their children. It drives me wild." Then she said, "We have to tell Brenda about Billy."

Alex sighed again. "I know. I've been thinking about what to say to her ever since I left Davidson's office."

"How about the truth as you heard it."

Alex looked at Sue, her eyes in shadow. "Only a few days now, huh, sweetie?"

"Yep." She could not slow the days passing. Nothing would change the court date she dreaded. She met Alex's gaze with a troubled look. "I'm not ready, Alex."

Alex squeezed her hand and released it. "You'll be okay."

"I'm not so sure about that."

"Three-day weekend coming up."

"Without Cassie."

"Let's do something different," Alex suggested, her eyes on the fading colors of sunset.

"What?"

"Maybe go somewhere."

But they couldn't leave Brenda. She was too devastated by the news. "He built this garage out of guilt?" she asked as they speculated on Billy's motives.

"We're judging him," Sue said. "He's not here to defend himself."

Alex spoke with unexpected anger. "No, because he ran off. You don't disappear if you're innocent," she added, knowing as she said it that this was not always true. The boy had betrayed her trust and belatedly she was reacting to it.

"You do when you're scared. Come on, Alex, you know better than that," Sue said. "Everyone thinks he did it. I'd probably run too."

While Alex struggled with her own angry disappointment, Sue sank deeper into gloom as the coming week drew closer.

VI

After talking with the Family Court Commissioner, an immensely heavy man named Doug Donovan, Sue was no more enlightened on what would happen with custody than she had been when they arrived at the courthouse. Ted sat with her in the hallway as they waited for Cassie.

"If it goes beyond this, we might have to take it to another county," he said, breaking the uncomfortable silence between them.

She glared at him. "Why?" But she thought she knew; his law practice was here.

"Conflict of interest. I know the judges." He stood up, his hands rattling change in the pockets of his elegantly tailored suit.

She wondered what Cassie was saying to the heavy-set man whose jowls jiggled when he talked and whose eyes were set so deep in his face they were almost lost in the surrounding flesh. She crossed her legs and noticed Ted staring at the open V of her blouse. Involuntarily, she covered the area with one hand and he looked away.

After what seemed an interminable time, Cassie emerged from the room and frowned at her parents. Sue took note of the scowl and speculated about the cause.

That was it. No decisions made. Instead, another appointment when both parents would meet together with Donovan was set for next week.

"We'll stay at our new house this weekend," Ted remarked to their daughter.

Cassie said nothing. She grasped neither parent's hand as she walked between them toward the courthouse door.

Summer had arrived on the heels of Memorial Day weekend. Breathing deeply, Sue looked up at the intensely blue sky littered with puffy white clouds and welcomed the warm sunny day. All shades of green dominated the landscape of trees, bushes, grass — accented by black tree trunks and brightly colored flowers. A blue jay screamed nearby and a squirrel chattered at them from the same tree.

"See you Friday," Ted said as he leaned over and kissed Cassie goodbye.

"You okay, honey?" Sue asked when they were alone in the Tempo.

Cassie stared out the window, apparently not ready to talk. "Yes, Mama."

Sue left Cassie at Kiddie Kare and drove to Chancelor High. This was the last week of school. Next Monday she would turn into the office those things which belonged to the school. Then summer would begin for her.

The next day softball season ended, when Alex's team lost the first game during regionals. Alex gathered her girls together, along with Ben and Cassie, and talked to them. She told them she was pleased with their improved playing ability, their enjoyment of the game, their good sportsmanship. She said she would probably not be coaching next year but that it was nice to end the season with a team like this one. It was all true, her satisfaction with the season marred only by Billy James' downfall and disappearance.

Billy was still gone, and Alex half-hoped he wouldn't return. She did not know what she would say to him or that she wanted to say anything to him again.

The three of them stopped for deli, dropped the truck off at the apartment, and drove the Tempo to the lake to picnic. They settled at an isolated table near the water and watched the boats and sailboards while they munched on sandwiches.

Cassie had said little since talking to Donovan. It was as if she were lost in a world of her own, and Sue, Alex knew, was trying not to intrude.

"Are you disappointed?" Sue asked Alex.

"About the game, you mean?" Sue nodded, her mouth filled with tuna sandwich. "Yes and no. It would have been nice to go to State just once. You know?" Then, looking at Cassie, she asked in a whisper, "What's with her? Do you know?"

"Nope. I won't ask, either."

Cassie stood on a rock near the water, her back to them. A breeze ruffled her dark hair, lifting it away from her shoulders.

"I never knew her to be so quiet."

"Must have been something Donovan said or did yesterday."

"Did he ask anything about us?"

"Some things. Were we discreet and stuff like that. One of the things he asked was what I thought was most important for Cassie."

"What did you say?"

"Balance," Sue remarked, swallowing the last of her sandwich and starting on the chips.

"Nice answer." Cassie had made her way back to the table. "Hungry, kiddo?" Alex asked.

"I want some pop."

"There's milk for you." Sue brushed the hair back from Cassie's face and started to wipe the crumbs from her daughter's mouth.

Cassie took the napkin from her mother and smeared her face with it, then turned toward Sue. "I don't want milk. Mama, Mr. Donoway asked if I want to live with Daddy."

Sue's heart clenched painfully. "Donovan," she corrected. "Well, do you?"

"Can't I have some Pepsi?" Then, "I love Daddy."

"I know you do. Your dad knows it too," Sue said, hoping Cassie wouldn't think she had to choose between her parents.

"I like weekends with Daddy."

Sue thought she knew what Cassie was trying to say and said encouragingly, "I'm sure you do."

"I wanna stay with you and Alex, Mama." Cassie spoke hesitantly, with a glance toward Alex across the table.

Sue's heart expanded and she took a deep breath. "And we want you to stay with us." Her steady, calm tone belied her feelings even as a grin spread across her face. "Did you tell Mr. Donovan that?"

"I told him I like living with Daddy too." She shoved a handful of chips into her mouth.

"You didn't say you wanted things to stay as they are?"

"I said I liked living with you, too."

Sue could only glean from Cassie's words that she had shown no preference toward where she lived. That probably would work against her staying with her mother. But she couldn't coach the child, could she? Could she tell her what to say?

Now low in the west, the sun spread colors in all directions which turned the restless surface of the lake different shades of red. Jets trailed pink lines behind them, brush strokes across the sky. Boats slowly made their way to the marina, and sailboards and jet skis were loaded up and driven away. Waves slapped rhythmically against the shore. From a dense woods near the cliffs deer stepped into the clearing and stood like alert statues until Cassie pointed, whereupon they turned, flashed white tails, and vanished into the trees. A sliver of moon curved among glowing stars in the darkening sky.

Eventually, when daylight was completely gone, they packed up and made their way to the Tempo. Reluctant to leave the soothing beauty the park offered, Sue slowly turned the car toward home. "Nice way to spend an evening," she said quietly.

"Yes," Alex agreed. Then she said, "I got through it."

"What?" Sue asked, her thoughts back to the custody battle.

"The letter. I made it through these weeks."

"We both did. Do you think Mrs. Westover wrote it?"

"I don't know. Sometimes yes, sometimes no. I thought at first she wrote it, but I don't think she knows us well enough to have written some of that stuff."

"I wondered about that too. Whoever wrote it knew us pretty well."

"I suppose she could have found out. She's pretty chummy with Lisa Gavinski. I even considered Lisa as a possible suspect, but Lisa doesn't know us well either."

"Found out what?" Cassie asked from the back seat.

So they had to stop talking about it. "About our camping trip, kiddo."

"Are we going camping soon?"

"Well?" Having made the suggestion, Alex turned to Sue for confirmation.

"I guess we'll have to now," Sue said, remembering the few times they had camped last summer.

The following Wednesday Ted and Sue met in Donovan's office. Sue wore a fitted suit and smelled pleasingly of cologne. Her face was tastefully made up — light earth-tone shadows on her eyelids, eyelashes slightly darkened and thickened, a touch of rouge and lipstick. She wanted to give off an aura of femininity to counter any of the illusions the word *lesbian* might conjure in Donovan's mind.

She read approval of her appearance in Ted's eyes. Not that she cared, she told herself. And she thought she saw an appreciative glimmer from the recesses of Donovan's gaze, about which she cared even less. She shuddered slightly.

"Are you cold?" Donovan asked solicitously.

"No, I'm fine, thank you." She glanced around the cheerless room with its plain wooden table, straight chairs, and unadorned windows.

"I brought you here to see if together you could reach a suitable agreement concerning your daughter's custody. She seems to have no preference for one of you over the other."

Oh, but she does, Sue almost said. But how could she prove Cassie had said as much? "Are you certain she just doesn't want to admit she prefers living with one parent over the other?" she heard herself ask.

The big man looked at her and blinked. A huge roll of flesh bulged over his shirt collar. She wondered about his social life. Did he have a girlfriend, a boyfriend? What did he do in his spare time? He must do more than eat.

"That can be a problem, but not usually with one so young as Cassie. Do you think that has happened here?"

"Yes, I do," Sue said.

"The point here is that I can give her a real home, heterosexual role models, a healthy lifestyle. I don't want my daughter to grow up emulating lesbians."

"You do not deny that you are in a homosexual relationship?" Donovan turned his gaze on Sue for affirmation.

"No, but I don't expect my daughter to assume my sexual orientation. Such preferences are established early in life," she said, thinking they sounded like talking textbooks. Perhaps Donovan would be impressed.

"Like around six years old," Ted put in.

"That's not a proven fact."

Sue didn't know what made a child prefer one sex over the other or when that orientation was cemented in the child's psyche. "I would never try to influence her one way or the other."

"The way you live influences her," Ted remarked in that cool, superior tone that annoyed her so much.

"I know she's happy with me. She said as much a week ago. She doesn't want to hurt her father's feelings by admitting she wants to spend most of her time with me. Nothing has ever been established that a parent's sexual orientation influences his or her child." Sue felt desperate.

"That leaves a reasonable doubt, and if there's such a doubt, the child should stay with the parent who provides the most acceptable home life," Ted countered.

Ted was nearly convincing Sue, who became more irritated every time he spoke. She wanted to argue whose lifestyle was healthier. Was it only sexual orientation that mattered? "You're talking about only one facet of her home life. There are so many other things that are equally important or even more so. I give her love and attention and discipline. I'm there for her every day. As I remember, Ted didn't get home from the office oftentimes until seven at night and he spent many Saturdays working. When he did come home, he buried himself in the paper or television. He had little time for Cassie."

"It's not that way anymore," Ted said, his eyes on her. He actually sounded sorry.

"I don't think we're getting anywhere today," Donovan stated. "There's the Family Court Mediation Program and psychological evaluation, after which the court decides. We may have to move on to that."

"Good. Let's do it," Ted said, getting to his feet. "I have to get to court myself, Doug." He leaned over to shake Donovan's hand.

Unfair, Sue thought. He knew the man. "Maybe we should move this to another county," she said.

"I'll set things up." Donovan leaned on the table and struggled to his feet.

Sue's hand was lost in his grip, which was surprisingly dry and warm and firm. He smiled at her and she liked him better. She realized she had held his bulk against him and felt momentarily ashamed. In the hallway, she and Ted turned in different directions.

When they returned tired and dirty from a weekend of camping, they found Billy James waiting for them in his old truck. He was the last person Alex wanted to see and a glance at Sue told her that she felt the same, but Cassie was clearly excited by his presence.

"Billy, we went camping," Cassie shouted, as if the weekend had been a great success. Apparently forgotten were the sunburn, the rain, the night spent in the car.

He stepped out of his truck, his long legs encased in faded, torn jeans. He looked as if he had slept in his clothes. "Sounds like fun, squirt," he said, smiling at the girl. Then he turned a worried look on Alex.

Feeling ill-equipped to deal with anything more serious than drying out their camping gear and putting things away, she sighed at the sight of him. "Where have you been, Billy?

"Kin we talk?" He motioned toward his truck.

"Let me help Sue put things away. Then we can talk," she said tiredly.

Billy laid the wet tent over the brick patio wall to dry out. The sky was overcast and the air thick with dampness. The four of them unpacked the car in record time, and Sue urged Alex to go with Billy, to leave the putting away of food and drying of clothes to her. Frowning, Cassie stayed with her mother reluctantly, as Billy and Alex left.

After driving out to the lakeside cliffs, Alex and Billy walked along a path overlooking the vast body of water. Pristine blue, it stretched for miles on end; from the cliff, even large boats looked like toys on its surface. Alex longed to be aboard one of them, inhaling the smell of water, the warm breeze lifting her hair off her forehead. They entered a forest of second- or third-growth timber, the path under their feet cushioned with bark. Rock formations rose at the edge of the cliffs with deep crevasses washed out between them, creating stony outcroppings.

"Okay, Billy, what's going on?" she asked, breaking the long silence.

"The police are after me," he said abruptly, bending to pick up a dead branch and break off its smaller limbs.

"Yes, I know. Why did you run off?"

"They think I started that fire at Brenda's." He would not look at her. His gaze was toward the huge lake.

"Did you?"

"No," he said quickly.

"Do you know who did?"

"I can't tell you who."

"You're going to take the punishment for what someone else did?"

"I knew it was going to happen. I couldn't stop it."

"Why?"

"They were friends. They said Brenda was queer."

Alex stopped in her tracks. "So they burned her house down?" She felt personally assaulted.

He nodded, still looking away. "You know what it's like when you can't stop something?"

"I don't understand why you couldn't warn her if you couldn't stop it." Alex was angry. What a stupid reason for setting someone's house on fire. Of course, there could never be a good reason.

"It was like I was already a part of it, and I didn't know Brenda then. I went along to make sure no one burned with the house and that the barn didn't catch fire." He turned to look at Alex, his eyes slits in an expressionless face.

"So that's why you rebuilt the garage for almost nothing."

He nodded, mute, apparently unable to explain the events leading to the fire.

Quiet for a few moments, Alex asked in a tired voice, "Why are you telling me? I don't know what I can do for you."

He shrugged his shoulders. "I don't know either."

"Tell the police the truth."

"They ain't gonna listen to me," he said bleakly.

She looked into the steely eyes. "You want them to listen to me? Then you better tell me everything."

But according to him, there wasn't much more to tell.

When she returned from the police station where Billy had been detained for questioning, it was dark. She had called Sue and arranged for bail before she left. She felt certain that Billy was being truthful about his guilt by what she considered cowardly association.

At home, she found Sue curled up on the couch reading. But knowing Sue, she had probably been unable to concentrate on anything and had spent most of the evening pacing. She looked up and patted the cushion next to her. "Tell me," she demanded.

So she told her, then added, "But get this, Sue. This is the worst part. They set that fire because Brenda was gay."

Sue's face mirrored emotion — surprise, disbelief, anger. "He told you that?" Then she added, "Brenda called. Cassie told her Billy was here. You have to call her."

Sighing, feeling extraordinarily tired, as if she could barely move her limbs, Alex called Brenda and told her everything except why the fire was set. They would tell her that together in person.

Talking about herself had never been one of Sue's strong points. She was more comfortable listening, which was one of the reasons she was a good guidance counselor. Yet here she was blabbing about her feelings and thoughts to this woman. Sue was so glad it was a woman.

But when she first came into the office, she had been distressed, sleepless the previous night, worried about the outcome of the session. Presumably, Cassie's custody hinged on this woman's opinion.

She paused and took a second look at the

psychologist, Claire D'Aubisson, who faced her with hands clasped, rocking slightly in a desk chair. Sue had thought it an impressive name, but the bearer was an average-size person, neither tall nor heavy, with a dark wedge haircut and silver wire-rimmed glasses over large gray eyes. There was nothing threatening about her.

"What is the worst thing that could happen with all this?" D'Aubisson asked.

"I could lose primary custody."

"Would that be so bad for Cassie?"

"Yes, I think so. She told me she wanted to live with us."

"How does she get along with Alex? It is Alex?"

"Yes." Sue straightened in her chair and smiled, mentally seeing Cassie with Alex. "Alex is like another mother to her — caring, attentive. Sometimes Cassie prefers being with Alex to being with me."

"Cassie's father worries how your relationship with Alex will affect her." The gray eyes gazed steadily at Sue and she returned the look.

Annoyed, feeling herself blushing, Sue said, "The fact that my parents were heterosexual didn't keep me from being gay — it just put off the inevitable."

"Why do you think Cassie should live with you?"

"I lived with Ted for three years after Cassie was born. He paid little attention to her. In fact, he wanted a boy. But I don't think a boy would have made any difference. He was just too busy with his life. Only now is he wanting primary custody, probably because I'm happy with a woman. Not only that, he's a chauvinist and shouldn't be raising a little girl." A sudden flare of anger warmed her.

"You've told me why your daughter shouldn't live with her father, not why she should live with you."

Realizing this was true, Sue cleared her throat and shifted in her chair, rubbing the wooden arms with her thumbs, noticing that the edges had been rubbed bare. "I don't want her potential limited by her sex." Sue talked slowly, searching for the right words. "I think I can give her more self-assurance. I know her dad loves her but he thinks differently about women. Not that I'm going to push her or anything. I just want her to know anything's possible. And I love being with her, watching her grow and think and have fun. She's a part of me." Sue paused, shrugging, and changed tack. "Do you have children?"

Claire shook her head and smiled faintly, her dark features lighting up.

She's gay, Sue thought with sudden insight. She might need this woman if she lost Cassie.

After the session, she found Alex deeply involved in a novel, waiting in the truck outside the Health Center doors.

"How'd it go?" Alex asked.

Sue climbed into the truck. "She's gay. I'm sure of it."

"Who's gay?" Alex turned the key and the engine sprang to life. She pointed the Chevy toward home.

"The psychologist, Claire D'Aubisson. How'd you like that for a name? I think she talked to Ted already."

Alex took Sue's hand.

"I liked her." The landscape sped past them, flashes of color. "How's the book?" Sue asked.

"It's making me horny."

"So what else is new?"

Alex, a wicked grin on her face, placed one hand between Sue's legs, squeezed gently, and nearly drove into the ditch.

Just off the highway Sue caught sight of an abandoned brick house surrounded by new homes, a lonely reminder of past lives. There had been a similar house close to Sue's childhood home. Sunlight had shafted through broken windows, dust motes dancing in the rays. Floors had creaked in empty rooms. Sue had gone there with a girlfriend who kissed her, took down her pants and touched her. How old had she been? Twelve? Through her unresisting shock, her heart had hammered with excitement.

Years later she had frequented the old house with Ted. In one of the upstairs rooms she had lost her virginity on an itchy wool blanket spread over cold hard wood. There had been none of the excitement she had felt with the girlfriend, just the ungiving surface pounding her backside.

Smiling, she recalled her first time with Alex. Sliding off the couch onto a heap on the carpet, blood pounding, breathing ragged. Alex had bent to kiss her, triggering a reaction neither could stop. She recalled the softness of Alex's lips, the taste of her tongue, the feel of her hands — so insistent yet gentle and warm. Thrilled, she had responded as she never had with Ted.

Squeezing Alex's hand, she said, "Let's drive past Ted's new house. I want to see it."

There was no one in sight as they approached the two-story brick home set back at least three hundred feet from the road. Unwittingly, Sue slouched in the front seat. Young newly planted trees sprouted from the freshly sodded yard. The house, unmistakably new, rose blunt and raw from its bare foundation.

"Would you like a house on a few acres?" she asked Alex once they were past.

"Why'd you hide?" Alex asked.

"I wasn't hiding."

"Why'd you scrunch down like that?"

"I just didn't want him to know I wanted to see the house."

"I don't know why you did, and no, I don't want a place with an immense lawn. Someone would have to spend all her time mowing."

"Let's start looking, Alex."

"Let's go home and hit the sheets."

VII

Summer continued in a haze of heat. Alex rose early to run in the cool mornings. She loved her solitary runs. As soon as the blinds turned gray and edged with first light, her eyes opened. She lay quietly listening to the morning sounds: birds proclaiming their territory with song, a few vehicles starting engines or passing on the road, an occasional dog barking.

The sound of Sue's breathing, quiet and regular, caused her to turn to the woman lying close to her. Coppery-colored hair spread across the pillow. Thick eyelashes shadowed cheeks flushed from sun and sleep, a rosy nipple exposed. Alex smiled and pulled the sheet to Sue's neck and bent to kiss the smooth forehead before slipping out of bed and dressing soundlessly.

She let herself out the door and warmed up by loping slowly toward the river which flowed a dark blue-gray. Ducks and Canadian geese, muttering companionably, bobbed on its surface. Gulls overhead pierced the quiet with their screams. Webs joined bushes, drops of dew still glistening on their delicate strands. Squirrels, tails spinning, performed aerial acrobatics between trees. Someone released a large sailboat from its moorings and started the outboard motor that would propel the yacht through the river to the large lake beyond.

Alex had spoken to her parents a few days ago and the conversation returned to her mind. They had wanted her to visit them in Florida, along with her brother David. She had demurred but was now having second thoughts. They had suggested she bring Sue and Cassie with her. Had it been the dead of winter she would have been thrilled at the thought of a change in the weather.

It might not be such a bad idea, though. Flights to Florida would be cheap this time of year. She had mentioned the conversation to Sue and then dismissed it from her mind. She would bring it up again today.

Sue squeezed her eyes more tightly shut, determined to sleep longer. Sleep had eluded her these past few weeks and when it came, it was filled with unpleasant dreams which she thankfully forgot as soon as she awakened.

Ted had told her yesterday that he would forego seeking primary custody if Sue and Cassie stopped living with Alex. "You have no right to tell me how to live," she had protested angrily, but now she silently considered the proposition.

She had lived alone with Cassie after the divorce. It had been a lonely time with Cassie a toddler, an anchor weighing her down. She had started exercising at the Y because they offered childcare. She had thought she might meet other adults, make some friends with similar interests. She had met Brenda and then Alex and come face to face with her own homosexuality. This time she hadn't run from it.

She went to the kitchen and made coffee, watched it drip into the pot, then took her cup out to the patio. The warm morning closed around her and she remembered how in her youth she had fled from her need for women, ending up saddled with Ted. So unfair for both of them.

Now he wanted her to do without Alex, was forcing her to think seriously about it. She sipped the hot, black liquid without tasting. A slight breeze, soft and feathery, with the scent of roses, touched her face. She pulled her feet up under her and sighed just as Alex, drenched with sweat, appeared at the patio's screen door. "How was your run?" she asked.

"Okay. Lovely out, isn't it?" Alex slid open the door and sat down next to Sue. "Want to go to Florida?"

"I can't leave with this custody thing going on." Then because she didn't know how to say it, she blurted, "Ted said he'd give up the custody battle if you and I stopped living together."

The silence that followed dragged on for what seemed a long time. Alex stopped mopping her sweat with the small kitchen towel and sat perfectly still. Her face registered no surprise. "I guess I expected this to happen," she remarked.

"Nothing's happened."

"Not yet." Alex rose from her chair and stepped back into the living room. "I'm going to shower."

Sue followed, not knowing what to say, and climbed into the tub with her. "Don't run from me, Alex." Standing in the mist, just out of the reach of the spray, Sue ached inside. For the first time in years she was satisfied with her life and now she was being forced to make an impossible choice.

"I'm not." Alex opened her eyes and smiled bleakly. "What about the house you wanted to look for?"

Sue shrugged helplessly. "He's offering me Cassie." She crossed her arms and hugged herself.

"Big of him," Alex said dryly. "You really think you're going to lose the custody thing, don't you?"

"I can't take the chance."

"I can go to Florida and come back to Brenda's. But he means it forever, you know." Her blue eyes were brilliant, icy.

"Until she can decide where she wants to live."

"Won't that be when she's twelve years old? Six years from now."

Desolate, never having expected Alex not to resist, Sue nodded.

Plastered to the airport window, Cassie stood apart from her mother and Alex and David who clustered near the gate. The jet had taxied to the terminal and disgorged its passengers minutes ago. They waited for the announcement to board and when it came, Alex called Cassie to her. "Give me a hug, kiddo." Bending over the child, she hid the emotion choking her. "Take care of your mother."

" 'Bye, Alex. Can I go next time?"

"Sure. We'll all go." Alex straightened and looked at Sue almost angrily. She felt heavy with exhaustion and slightly out of control, because they had talked until nearly dawn.

Sue pulled Alex into a hug and quietly said, "We'll decide when you get back. Okay?"

"Yeah, sure."

"Ready, Alex?" David hovered by the gateway.

Alex turned to wave at Cassie, who stood pressed once more against the window looking out. Then she and David climbed the steps to the plane.

"Nice of you to take vacation for this," Alex remarked, buckling her seatbelt and looking through the little window toward the terminal. She could see Cassie and Sue. She was sick inside, nauseous, and her heart felt crushed and damaged. How could she just leave? Should she make it easy for Sue? She closed her eyes, wishing she could shut her mind to the words Sue had spoken. Brenda would agree to let her stay with her if she needed to, would probably be glad for the company.

"You look terrible, Alex," David said with concern, looking at the bruises under her eyes. "Something wrong?"

"I didn't sleep much last night."

"Sue looked just as bad. Hard to part?"

"Yeah." Especially when the parting might be permanent, she thought.

That Sue would even consider acceding to Ted's demands filled Alex with a cold rage. But now, with the jet thundering down the runway toward take-off, the anger diminished and she felt empty, alone, as if she had years to fill and no idea how to do it. Last night their arguing had solved nothing. Sue had been unwilling to reject unconditionally Ted's terms for abandoning the custody suit, even though she acknowledged them as unreasonable.

"He probably knows you have a good chance of retaining custody," Alex had said as they sat facing each other, cross-legged on the bed.

"I don't think I have any chance against him," Sue had replied.

And if Sue lost primary custody, Alex knew she would be blamed for talking her into turning down Ted's offer. So she had given up trying.

Alex and her family filled the vacation week with activities — a trip to Epcot Center, walks on the beach, deep-sea fishing, rounds of golf. The busier the better was Alex's thinking. She slept dreamlessly, worn out from exercise and sunshine. She and David sparred occasionally, but for the most part it was goodhearted, and Alex felt closer to him than ever before.

When they were airborne on the trip home, David said, "It blows my mind when I have a good time with the folks."

Alex, who had been watching the city recede from the window of the 737, turned to meet his eyes. "It's nice when they become friends, isn't it?"

Giving her a smile that baffled her, he pressed the button to recline his seat.

"Cassie with her dad?" Alex asked, throwing her bags into the trunk of Sue's car. A wall of tension hung between them even in their first moments of reunion. Alex resented the position she had allowed Sue to assume, that it was Sue who would decide whether they separated.

Sue unlocked the car doors and they lowered themselves into the hot interior. She glanced at Alex, gave her a hesitant smile. "Got a little fried, didn't you? Have a good time?"

"Terrific, for all of us. And how was your week?" She cracked open her window as Sue turned on the air conditioner.

"A little lonesome but interesting. I spent a lot of it with Brenda. Cassie's been with Ted most of the week. Brenda wanted us to eat there tonight, but I thought I'd keep you to myself."

Avoiding Sue's eyes, Alex asked, "Why?" even as she warned herself to keep her mouth shut. "Does that mean we're staying together?"

"Don't be so angry," Sue said, frowning. "Tell me, Alex, what would you do in my place?"

"I'd tell him to go fuck himself."

"Would you? And lose your kid?" Sue looked grim, her mouth drawn into a straight line.

"You're not going to lose Cassie," Alex said without conviction. How did she know Sue wouldn't lose her?

"I wish I could be sure of that."

"So what did you decide?" Alex persisted, tucking her sunburned hands under her armpits.

"Don't make it so hard, Alex," Sue pleaded.

Her hopes shattered, Alex looked away and blinked back tears. "I want to eat at Brenda's tonight. I need to talk to her."

After reconfirming the invitation with Brenda, Sue followed Alex around the apartment. "Guess who was at the Women's Center?" Sue and Brenda had gone there during Alex's absence.

Alex shot Sue an angry glance. "Who?" She laid her suitcase on the bed, unable to decide whether she should unpack. If she was leaving, maybe it would be better to go now.

"Lisa Gavinski," Sue said with the faintest of smiles.

"No kidding? Lisa? Are you sure?" Astonished, because she had been so sure Lisa was straight, she stared at Sue. "Did she recognize you?"

"Oh, sure. She asked where you were."

"Maybe she doesn't know that's a lesbian watering hole." Alex frowned in thought. "Do you think that's possible?"

Sue shrugged. "Anything's possible."

It was very unlikely, Alex realized. Opening her suitcase, she dropped the dirty clothes on the floor as Sue watched. "I'll throw them in the washer before we leave for Brenda's."

As they pulled up to the unfinished garage, they could see Brenda moving about the kitchen of her new house trailer. "Have you seen Billy?" Alex asked Sue, getting out of the truck and shutting the door. The evening felt cool and soothing, after the suffocating heat of Florida.

"Nope. I asked Brenda once if he'd been back to work on the garage and she said she hadn't seen him. Least he could do is finish it, don't you think?"

"Maybe I should suggest that to him."

Brenda opened the door and threw her arms around Alex. A faint odor of horse emanated from Brenda like perfume. "I missed you too," Alex said.

Over dinner, Alex recounted her trip, taking note of Brenda's questioning looks. Brenda must wonder why they were here her first night home. Refusing to allow herself to think, Alex pushed back her unhappiness. Once she glared at Sue and was met by a look so sad her rage dissipated.

Later in the evening, after several glasses of wine, Alex asked bluntly, "Do you want a roommate?"

"What?" Brenda said.

"Can I stay with you until I find a place?" Alex's voice faded on the last few words.

Brenda showed no surprise. "Sure, Alex," she said, eyeing one friend and then the other. "It'll be nice having someone around. But I wish this hadn't happened." Her voice broke and the three of them looked in different directions.

The next morning Alex packed. Sue had slept little, waking long before dawn and lying sleepless, knowing the other was less than an arm's length away.

As morning filtered light into the room, Sue reached for Alex. The lovemaking that followed was infinitely tender and made to remember. Closing her eyes, Sue had run her hands over Alex's slender body, tracing the long muscles, as if memorizing the curves and velvety skin. When her hand closed over the wiry mound of hair, she paused to hold it gently before exploring the familiar folds, wet and warm and silken. She shuddered when Alex responded with a hesitant touch — caressing, arousing, eliciting ecstasy, sustaining passion as only Alex knew how.

Now it was over and Alex, feeling drained from lack of sleep and too much emotion, threw clothes without care into several open suitcases on the unmade bed. She heard the apartment door open and Cassie's voice calling for her mother, the thud of small feet coming down the hall toward the bedroom. Knowing Sue was in the bathroom and sensing Cassie standing in the doorway, she turned. "Hi, kiddo. How you been?"

Cassie's hazel eyes widened. "Hi, Alex. Where are you going?"

"How about a hug and a kiss. I haven't seen you for over a week."

Cassie wrapped her small frame around Alex, who held the girl close. She looked up to see Sue standing in the room. When she set Cassie down, the child turned to her mother for answers. "Where's Alex going now?"

"To stay with Brenda for a while," Sue said.

"Why?" Then without waiting for a reply, "I want to go too."

The women's eyes met over Cassie's head and Alex waited for Sue to explain what was going on. It gave her a perverse satisfaction to see Sue in this bind, to listen to her attempts to answer Cassie's persistent "Why?"

Although she missed Sue fiercely, Alex suspected life at Brenda's was infinitely more interesting than it was for Sue at the apartment. She allowed herself little time for thought — only late at night before she fell asleep or early morning when she awoke alone. Some mornings she wanted Sue with an intensity that alarmed her, and her hand would steal between her legs seeking a solitary release. At night, though, she was usually so tired from barn work that she was spared desire. One night after they had cleaned down most of the stalls, it occurred to Alex that it was small wonder Brenda managed without sex.

She had the surprise of her life the following evening when Janice Henderson showed up at the door, bearing a bottle of wine. Janice was one of the homeliest people Alex had ever seen. A short woman, the antithesis of Brenda, what she lacked in beauty she compensated for with wit. Pretending she had a book she couldn't put down, Alex grabbed a sandwich and retired to her room to give the two women privacy. From behind the closed door she could hear their voices punctuated by laughter. Miserable, unable to concentrate, she lay on her bed and waited for sleep.

The following day she was up before six for her daily run, slipping out the door into the early July morning. Yesterday's heat rose off the pavement and surrounding fields, shrouding the low places in ground fog. Wheat, waving in the fields, stood nearly ready for harvest. Next to it yellow oats offered a pale contrast. Acres of alfalfa, richly green, bordered fields of corn. Alex thought the crops were beautiful. She looked forward to putting up hay with Brenda.

Running along the gravelly berm, noticing the wildflowers in the ditches, hearing the birds greeting the day with song, she felt somewhat compensated for her loss. She had talked to Sue once since the move to Brenda's, knew she would be coming to the barn with Cassie today.

Turning the corner onto Smith Road, she decided to run past Billy's farmhouse. Her feet softly scrunched on the small stones as she approached. One stark, tall fir tree drooped forlornly in the front yard. The Chrysler still crouched on cement blocks in the weedy driveway. Suddenly recalling the dog, she picked up speed. Perhaps he wouldn't hear her.

She was nearly past the house and beginning to consider herself safe when the dog's fierce bark shattered the quiet and flooded her system with adrenalin. She spied the animal bolting around the near corner of the house. Putting on a tremendous burst of speed, her backside prickling with the anticipation of attack, she sprinted for her life. Turning at the last moment to face the onslaught of furry fury, she heard Billy shout, "Pal!"

The dog skidded to a stop at her feet and, tongue dangling over yellow teeth, dripped saliva onto her shoes. Its golden-brown eyes darted from her to Billy who had started across the yard toward them. Billy placed a hand on the dog's head. "You just ain't met him is all. He's not a bad dog. Just don't like strangers." A grin lit up his pitted face.

Trembling and too relieved to be angry, Alex gasped for air. She had thought the dog meant to rip her to shreds. She glanced at the huge animal. "Why don't you tie him up?"

"Say hello to her, Pal," Billy commanded. "She's a nice lady. Got me out on bail." Pal's ears, framed by burrs, swiveled forward and his tail wagged slowly. "Give him a pat."

Hesitantly, Alex laid a hand on the dog's head and the animal licked her arm and whined. "Tell me he wouldn't have torn me up and spit me out." She glanced at Billy.

"He might of took off a little skin is all, nothing serious." He looked amused. His hair, cut short enough to stand up in spikes, gave him a slightly more respectable appearance. "He's a good guard dog."

And what were they guarding? Alex wondered. There didn't appear to be anything worth stealing — the lawn mower still rusting in the yard, a rototiller in the middle of a weed-infested garden. "You never finished Brenda's garage," Alex said accusingly, suddenly angry. Her heart had just slowed to a normal beat.

"I'll get to it." He glanced at his bare feet, which were terribly white and oddly defenseless-looking.

"When?"

"Soon. It ain't so easy going back there, you know." He gave her what she thought was a pleading look. "How do I know she won't run me off?"

"Take Pal with you," Alex suggested and they laughed.

Sue's week had been terrible. She couldn't remember such loneliness. Had she felt so alone after her marriage ended? She thought not, because Ted had left her lonely even when he was around. Alex's absence made a huge hole in her life that she didn't know how to fill.

Cassie had been crabby and difficult. Now she was so excited at the prospect of going to the barn that Sue had to send her back to her room three times, reminding her that she couldn't ride in shorts or tennis shoes and she needed her helmet.

They located Brenda near the tack room, helping youngsters with their mounts. "Go get Shorty, Cassie," Brenda said. Cassie obediently trotted off down one of the aisles.

"Does she need help?" Sue asked, her eyes on Cassie's back.

"Naw, she'll be fine. How are you?" Brenda handed the reins of a black and white pinto to a girl and sent her to the arena to warm him up. "You look tired."

"It's awful, Brenda." Hearing her own voice, low and trembling, Sue struggled to pull herself together. After all, she had been the one to ask Alex to leave. "Maybe it'll get better."

"Sure it will," Brenda said with a false heartiness. She squeezed Sue's shoulder in a painful grip.

Sue brushed away a few stray tears with the back of her hand. "Where's Alex?" she asked, opening the door to the lounge.

"Somewhere mucking out a stall. She'll show up. She wants to see you as much as you want to see her."

Somehow Sue doubted the truth of that statement.

Billy James and Alex appeared at the same time, Billy's truck trailing a plume of dust as Alex emerged from the barn and blinked in the pale sunlight. Bits of sawdust and hay clung to her, stuck to her clothing and the prickling sweat on her bare skin.

She noticed Billy and then Sue, who was sitting on the bench outside the barn holding Tabby on her lap. Her heart leaped at the sight of Sue. She almost smiled but swallowed the impulse.

Billy hesitated, one foot on the rear bumper of

his truck, hands in back pockets. His face appeared less narrow, less dangerous — almost boyish, Alex thought — with the shorter hair.

"Good to see you, Billy," Alex said. "Where's Pal?" She allowed herself a brief smile.

"Home. Didn't think you wanted to see him." He nodded at Sue. "How you doing?"

"Good. Going to work on the garage?"

"Yes ma'am, and whatever else needs done." He waved at Cassie and Brenda and strode on long legs toward the garage.

That left Sue and Alex alone. Alex turned her gaze on Sue. "You had your hair cut." Sue's thick, coppery head of hair turned under just below her ears.

Her eyes softened with longing at the sight of Alex, as if Alex's anger was better than no emotion at all. Alex crossed her arms. Sue crossed her own tanned arms, and as Alex watched, Sue smiled.

Alex's frown deepened. "What's so amusing?"

Shaking her head, Sue said, "It's just good to see you."

"Humph," was the reply. But Alex hadn't known how much she missed Sue until she saw her. She hungered for her, longed to just touch her arm. "So, how's it going?"

"I never thought it would be so lonely without you or I couldn't have let you go."

"But you did." Was this an invitation to return? Alex wondered.

"I had to, Alex." Sue squinted against the sun's rays filtering through the long line of clouds. "Can we see each other once in a while?"

"We're seeing each other now."

"Can you spend the night when Cassie's at her dad's?" Sue shielded her eyes with one hand, looked intently at Alex.

What a temptation, Alex thought, softening a little. Should she hold out against it? All or nothing? "When's that going to be?" she heard herself ask.

"Tomorrow."

Alex placed one foot on the bench. "We're putting up hay tomorrow if it doesn't rain. I'll be beat."

"Maybe I can help," Sue volunteered.

"That's up to you and Brenda." Alex shrugged, pretending not to care.

Tabby had purred loudly through the entire conversation under Sue's absentminded stroking. But in the ensuing silence, they distinctly heard the purrs, Billy hammering, Brenda calling instructions to the riders, horses blowing dust from their nostrils and the beat of hooves on the hard ground.

The riders dismounted and made their way back to the barn, Cassie stopping to accuse her mother and Alex on the way, "You didn't watch me."

"We were talking." Sue didn't deny it.

"Go on, Cassie, and brush him good after you untack," Brenda said, encouraging the child with a pat on the back.

When Alex stuck her head out the door early the next morning, she raised her face to a cloudless sky. The sun had already burned away whatever dew was left, promising a day windless and hot. She looked forward to it — to working outside with Sue. And Brenda and Billy, she reminded herself. She had never baled hay but had seen tractors pulling wagons with people on them stacking bales. It had looked like fun.

Yesterday, when Billy had asked if Brenda needed help putting up hay, Brenda had given him a glare and a curt nod and turned away. Alex had seen him look down and rub a toe in the dirt of the driveway and wondered if he would indeed show up.

By eight-thirty the chores were done, and she and Brenda grabbed a bite to eat while waiting for Sue and, hopefully, Billy. Baling wouldn't begin until the cut hay was dry. Sue arrived about nine, just before Billy, who looked ready to work.

In the field across the road, Brenda drove the tractor and baler that shot the bales onto the wagon. Sue balanced on the slowly moving wagon, throwing the sixty-pound bales to Alex and Billy who stacked them in rows starting at the rear of the flat wagon and working toward the front, climbing higher as the load grew.

Toward noon they broke for lunch, first dousing themselves in the hundred-gallon water tank, then wolfing down sandwiches and quarts of water. Sue moved her arms gingerly, as if to ease the ache. Alex, who thought she was in good shape, had never sweated so much. She flexed her shoulders and felt the strain.

"It's time to unload these wagons," Brenda said. "Then maybe Sue'd like to drive the tractor for a while."

In the high empty loft of the barn Brenda and Billy stacked the hay that Sue placed on the hay elevator as Alex threw the bales off the wagons.

When the wagons were empty, they returned to the field and again began baling. With Sue on the tractor, Alex threw the bales to Brenda and Billy who stacked.

The relentless sun burned through the film of dust and bits of hay plastered to their drenched bodies. Sweat dripped into their eyes and lured sweat bees that stung with a ferocity unequal to their minute size.

They put the last bale in the loft as night offered a cooling hand. In the camaraderie created by work, Brenda seemed to have forgiven Billy, and he resumed his easy-going manner.

"Well, ladies, you done good," he remarked, brushing himself off before getting into his truck. "I'll be back tomorrow to work on the garage. Okay?" He peered at Brenda in the growing dark.

Stars appeared in the blackening sky and the moon rose full and red. The three women lay on the sparse grass outside the trailer and watched the overhead display. Hundreds of fireflies flickered in the darkness. A whippoorwill called repeatedly and was repeatedly answered. The night deepened and still they didn't leave it. The moon lost its red color and shed a golden path across the barnyard.

Finally Brenda said, "I hope you brought a change of clothes, Sue."

"I did."

"I'm going to shower and then we'll order a pizza. Thanks, you two. Couldn't have done it without you. You saved me some money today. Last year I hired help."

"It was fun," Sue remarked.

"That's because you were driving the tractor most of the time while we were wrestling sixty-pound bales of hay," Alex pointed out.

"True. I had the easy job."

"I don't think I ever worked harder in my life," Alex remarked. "I know where every muscle is."

"Want a rub?" Sue asked, lying flat with arms outstretched.

Alex paused before refusing in a low voice. "I'll be all right." She had given agonizing thought to Sue's suggestion that they spend nights together when Cassie was gone. It seemed like cutting off her nose to spite her face, but she couldn't do it. She couldn't allow herself to be convenient. She had to be more than that to Sue.

Getting her overnight bag out of her car, Sue took it into the trailer and showered after Brenda. Realizing Alex wasn't going to join her, she hurried the process. Brenda had a drink waiting for her when she emerged from the bathroom and Alex took her place.

"Doesn't it feel good just to sit?" Brenda fell onto the sofa and patted the cushions, urging Sue to join her. "What's going on between you two?"

Sue curled up in a corner, pulling her bare feet up under her, sipping on the gin and tonic Brenda had made.

"Nothing. I could stay the night, Brenda, or she could spend it with me at the apartment. I don't think she's going to let that happen. She's too angry, and I don't blame her. I would probably feel the same way."

"She'll get over it. Stay anyway. There are three bedrooms. If she won't let you sleep with her, sleep in the spare room."

Sue was quiet, thinking it might be unbearable to be under the same roof and in a different bed than Alex. "Tell me about you? Alex said Janice was here the other night."

Brenda's face flushed and an embarrassed grin spread across it. "There's nothing to tell."

"You don't look like there's nothing to tell." Sue smiled at Brenda's confusion. Her own loneliness did not prevent her from wanting more for her friend.

"She's coming out here tomorrow night," Brenda admitted.

"Good. Then Alex and I should get out of your hair, just disappear for a while."

"No. I want you both here for dinner," Brenda said firmly. "Then maybe you can go to the apartment." She looked pleadingly at Sue as if to say: Don't leave me alone.

That night when Sue stood by the side of Alex's bed and asked to join her, Alex did not say no. Instead she rolled as close as she could to one side without falling on the floor, showed her back to Sue, and fell asleep. Exhausted, Sue curled around her former lover, sighed in partial contentment, and drifted into sleep. In the morning Alex was gone from the bed when Sue awakened.

VIII

The ringed moon hung low in the eastern sky when Sue drove to Ted's house to pick up Cassie Sunday evening, making her wonder if rain was in the offing. She stood on the porch of the large brick house after ringing the doorbell. Now perhaps she would meet Jean.

Cassie flung the door open and leaned out. "Hi, Mama."

Sue bent and gave her daughter a brief hug and kiss. Cassie pulled Sue into the slate-floored foyer, and Sue caught a glimpse of herself in the long mirror just inside the door. Having spent the weekend at Brenda's, she wore jeans and sweatshirt and tennis shoes. She hoped she didn't smell like a horse.

"Come on, Mama." Cassie dragged her mother into the living room.

Sue felt awkward, and resisted intruding into her ex-husband's life. "Cassie, why don't you get your things and we'll go home?" But then she found herself in the living room with Ted, who had his arm around a younger woman. So this was Jean.

Ted introduced them and Jean stood as they exchanged greetings.

The two women were about the same height, but Sue thought Jean weighed a good ten pounds less than she did. A little disconcerted, she made an effort to look around and show some interest in the new house. "You have a lot of room here." The living room had to be at least thirty feet long with huge bay windows looking out on the backyard. There was an immense fireplace with a deep mantle, thick beige carpeting, new furniture, and a few paintings on the off-white walls.

"Would you like to see the house?" Jean asked.

"Oh, no thanks, not tonight anyway," she said hastily, looking from Jean to Ted, noticing his lazy smile. Smug? she wondered. But she wouldn't want to live in this house. She knew that before she even walked into it. *Pretentious* was the word she would use to describe it. She placed an arm around Cassie's shoulders. The familiar feel of her daughter's body brought Sue comfort.

Cassie clutched a squirming orange striped cat in her arms. "See, Mama. This is Tiger." Tiger stared at Sue out of untamed yellow eyes, then jumped out of the child's arms and bounded out of the room. "He's not friendly. He bites." She pointed to small indentations on her arm.

"We had his claws pulled. We'll get him neutered soon. Maybe he'll be friendlier then," Ted said, almost apologetically.

"I hope so." Sue started toward the door, contemplating the barbaric things people did to animals to make them acceptable pets. "Got your suitcase, sweetie?"

"I'll get it." Cassie ran out of the room and returned with her bag banging against her leg, the sleeve of a shirt hanging out the side.

The apartment smelled stale, as if no one lived there. Sue switched on lights and opened the patio door, then turned on the radio for company. Surveying the room, she realized belatedly and with a sense of relief how much Alex had left behind, as if she only planned a brief absence. "Come sit with me, honey, and tell me about your weekend," she said.

Cassie climbed up on the sofa next to her mother. "We planted flowers and stuff and I played with Heather. Heather lives next door and she's bossy. Did you go to the barn?"

"We put up hay Saturday."

"Aw, Mama, I wanted to help."

"You're really too little. I was almost too little. The hay probably weighs more than you do." Cassie pondered that notion. Sue realized it might never have occurred to the child that her mother could be too small for anything. "Want to read before you go to bed?"

During the night Sue tore the sheets and blanket from the bed in her restless quest for sleep. Toward morning, when thunder and lightning split the darkness, Cassie climbed into bed with her, pulled the covers over her head, and they both slept.

The sheets of rain Monday morning were thoroughly depressing. Her mother called late in the morning.

"It's dreadful out, isn't it? Want to go shopping? It's been too long since I saw you and Cassie."

"I'll pick you up, Mom. Give me an hour."

While they walked the mall, Sue told her mother that Alex had moved to Brenda's and why. Her voice shook a little as she explained. Cassie had gone ahead of them.

"It must be lonely for you," Joanne said.

"Those aren't strong enough words," Sue said.

"So, you agreed to Ted's conditions?" her mother asked.

"Yes. What would you have done?"

"Don't ask me that. I probably wouldn't have left Ted in the first place." They paused to look in a store window. "I like Alex, Sue, but maybe this is for the best. You have to think about Cassie."

"What do you mean?" Sue girded herself for verbal battle, but her mother's tone was conciliatory.

"Don't get all huffy, dear. You have to set a good example for Cassie."

"We always set a good example for her."

"Honey, this isn't something I want to discuss in

depth," Joanne said. "It does seem better to me this way is all."

"Okay, Mom. We won't talk about it."

Cassie worked her way between them, ending the discussion.

"Got the hay in just in time," Brenda remarked Monday morning, coffee cup in hand, staring out the trailer window at the drenching rain. Spurts of mud splashed with each droplet and steam rose from the ground.

"When did Janice leave?" Alex asked, sitting at the table in shorts and T-shirt. The hot coffee burned her tongue and throat.

"An hour or so after you and Sue left us alone." Brenda continued to watch the rain. "Why did you do that?"

"Sue had to leave and I thought you might want to be alone."

"What for?"

Exasperated, Alex replied, "For whatever, Brenda. So you could get to know each other better." Alex looked at Brenda's profile, thinking that it took time to get used to someone else.

"It was so obvious, Alex." Brenda turned slowly, showing Alex a tired face.

"Sorry. Do you care for Janice?"

"You mean, do I care enough to jump into bed with her? Why didn't you ask me that yesterday?" She turned away.

When she didn't continue, Alex asked, "Well, do you?"

"I'm not ready for that. I don't know if I'll ever be ready."

"The first moves might be hard, Brenda. After that it gets easier."

"Somebody has to make the first moves."

Alex stood and stretched, then laid an arm across Brenda's broad shoulders. "You can do it," she said.

A brief smile flitted across Brenda's face. "Then so can you."

"That's different," Alex muttered.

"No, it's not. Why not take what you can get? That's what you're saying to me."

Alex frowned in thought. "We had a relationship. Sue wants to keep selected parts of it. I want the whole thing. You're just sticking your feet in the water to see what it feels like. You can't know what you want until you taste it."

"My, aren't we eloquent this morning?" Brenda's grin lifted her features.

Lightly punching her friend on the shoulder, Alex said, "Go ahead, make fun of me."

"I think it's all the same." Her grin warmed Brenda's pale blue eyes, lifted the corners of her generous mouth. "My mother used to say don't throw away the choice pieces with the bad."

One hot day followed another. The thermometer seemed stuck in the high eighties and nineties and one day reached one hundred degrees. The barn buzzed with fans. Brenda bought old furnace blowers and set them in the aisles to keep the air moving and, along with it, the dust. The flies were dispatched with a mister. If the mist killed the flies, Alex argued, what must it be doing to their lungs? Brenda said she'd rather take a chance with the mist than put up with flies.

Sue spent most days at the barn too, pitching in with the work. The nights Cassie went to Ted's, Sue stayed in Brenda's trailer. Alex had never said no when Sue asked to sleep with her and finally gave up her resolve to abstain from sex. She had been able to resist the feel of Sue against her only so long, had steeled herself against Sue's gentle touch for that short length of time. She told herself, when she turned over and reached for Sue one hot night, that maybe Brenda had been right, that she had been hurting herself as much or more than Sue.

"Goddamn you," she said, and grabbed Sue in a fierce embrace. Her lovemaking was rough and quick, reflecting angry frustration.

As July drew to a close, Sue suggested a camping trip with Alex. Cassie would be with Ted for the first two weeks in August. Sue and Alex could travel around the state, staying at different campgrounds.

"You act like nothing's happened," Alex said. Her anger flared whenever Sue unwittingly said the wrong thing, throwing fuel on an inner flame.

"I don't know how else to behave," Sue countered. "Wouldn't it be nice to get away, go to a lake together?"

"And then come back to you and Cassie at the apartment and me here?"

"It could be worse. We are at least together much of the time."

"We're going backwards, Sue. Can't you see that?

School will start. Then when will we see each other? I don't want a weekend romance."

In the end she relented; even a couple weeks alone with Sue were better than none. When they returned, volleyball practice would begin for Alex and both women would be embroiled in school meetings.

After a few days on the road, staying at various campgrounds, Alex paused outside the camp office by a pay phone. "Think we should call Brenda?" she asked hesitantly, reluctant to bring even Brenda into their private world.

"Probably. I should call Ted, too, and see how Cassie is."

The phone rang distantly in Alex's ear. She counted the rings, picturing the interior of the barn. Brenda always told her to let it ring at least ten times. It made Brenda furious to run for the phone and have the caller hang up.

"Alex! Am I glad to hear your voice."

"Why, Brenda? Something wrong?"

"Yes, something's very wrong. Billy's been shot. He's in the hospital. I'm scared, Alex. Whoever shot him probably was the one that torched the house."

Thrust back into the real world with Brenda's words, Alex's shoulders sagged. "We'll come home today."

That evening Alex pushed through Billy's hospital room door and walked toward his bed. She had never seen such pale, pitted skin. His hair lay lank and dirty, staining the white pillowcase. Layered with gauze, his shoulder and leg looked misshapen. His lids fluttered, then opened wide. His eyes, momentarily startled, became narrow and guarded.

"Hi, Billy." She attempted a smile.

"Thought you were on vacation." His voice sounded reedy and thin.

"I was. Then I heard about you and thought I'd better come home. What happened?"

The gray eyes looked opaque. "I don't know."

"You were in a heap of trouble before. Now you're in danger and you still won't talk. Guess I can't help you then."

"You shouldn't be here. Anyone seen you come in?"

"I don't think so." It hadn't occurred to her that she risked danger by association.

"Go away. You're right, you can't help me."

"Tell the police, Billy."

He gave her a strange, shuttered look and turned away before saying in a soft voice, "I don't want your help. You're queer."

It felt like a slap. Had he spat at her, her reaction might have been the same. Backing away from the bed, she turned and quickly fled the room. Shocked and hurt, she followed the lines on the floor leading out of the hospital.

That evening Alex discussed Billy with Sue and Brenda while sitting outside the trailer.

Sue had definite ideas about Billy's deliberate insult. "Don't you see, Alex? He said that to get you out of there."

"It got me out all right. I nearly ran."

"I don't think he cares whether you're queer or I'm queer," Brenda said, a shadow in the dark.

"He's afraid for you, Alex." Sue leaned forward. "That's scary."

"Then he thinks he's still in danger," Alex said.

The other two women nodded.

They sent Billy flowers along with a card and a carefully worded note by Alex urging swift recovery. Unable to bring herself to comment on his rude remark, she ignored it.

The laziness of summer ended for Alex with volleyball practice in mid-August. Many of the returning players had been on her softball team, including Michelle, Ginger, Kelly.

After the first practice, Alex drove Michelle home and went on to Billy's house. She saw him sitting in a chair in the yard, his bad leg resting on a crate. Breathing deeply for courage, she cut the engine and stepped out of the truck.

Pal, who had risen from a prone position to his haunches when Alex drove onto his property, leaped into a run as soon as her feet touched the ground. He dropped in obedience at her command to sit, and Billy applauded from his chair. When she walked toward Billy through the tall scraggly grass, the dog followed with his nose in her palm. Placing a hand on his head, she felt the burrs around his ears and tugged gently at one. He took the offending hand in his mouth.

"He don't like to be groomed," Billy remarked with a weak smile, his face ghostly. "Want to sit?" With one hand, he started to lift himself out of the chair.

"No thanks."

"Don't you know better than to be seen with me?" As if to emphasize that worry, he looked down the road both ways.

"You want me to stay away?" she asked, still patting the dog's head.

"He'll pester you to death if you keep that up. Lie down, Pal."

"I don't mind. It's better than being mauled." She smiled faintly.

And he grinned, then looked away. "Sorry about what I said at the hospital. I'd say it again, though, but I know it won't do no good. It won't keep you away."

"I know, Billy. Why don't you just talk to the police?"

He looked directly in her eyes. "I can't. It goes against the grain. You know?"

"Getting shot goes against the grain too, and it can be fatal."

He shrugged. "You gonna help me this fall? I still gotta get six credits to graduate."

"Sure, Billy. Come to the barn when you feel better."

"It's better I don't."

"I'll come see you again soon." She picked her way through the cluttered, unkempt yard to her truck. " 'Bye, Pal," she called over her shoulder.

The dog came instantly to her side and escorted her to the truck, leaning against her leg.

Back at Brenda's, she announced, "Billy's home." She stood near the tack room patting Shorty who was cross-tied in the aisle.

"That so? How's he doing?" Brenda leaned against the wall putting together a bridle.

Cassie stood on a wooden box, brushing Shorty's dusty coat of hair vigorously. The tip of her tongue touched her upper lip in concentration.

Brenda glanced down the aisle at the other girls grooming their horses. "Go ahead and tack up," she called. "Want to help with the bridles, Alex?" Pointing a thumb at Shorty's long-backed, short-legged, large-bellied body, Brenda remarked, "Do you believe I've got someone who wants to buy him?"

"You're gonna sell Shorty?" Cassie said, outraged. "He's mine."

"You can ride something else, Cassie," Brenda said.

"I don't wanna ride something else." She turned with a scowl as if to walk away and Brenda grabbed her and lifted her onto Shorty.

"Okay, I won't sell him. Lead the crew out of here now." Brenda walked with the line of girls as some rode, some led their mounts out of the barn, leaving Sue and Alex behind.

Cassie's two weeks with her dad were over, so she and Sue were back at the apartment. Alex, having gotten used to Sue sharing her bed, was in a sulk. She stuffed her hands in her back pockets and glared at Sue. "I'm going to clean stalls while the school horses are out of them."

"I'll help," Sue said eagerly.

Working in adjoining stalls, they shared a wheelbarrow and talked through the bars separating the top halves of the stalls. Alex threw sawdust and manure at the wheelbarrow, dumping as much on the floor as in it. "It's no good, Sue. I don't want to do this anymore." She jabbed angrily at a pile of wet sawdust, which smelled strongly of ammonia.

"Do what?" Sue asked anxiously, leaning on her pitchfork.

"I don't want to be so available. It makes me feel cheap."

Sue dropped her pitchfork and closed the distance between them to shove a surprised Alex against the wall. She said, "I won't insult you anymore if that's what you think I'm doing. I'd take you right here, though, if you'd let me, and it wouldn't be because you're convenient. It'd be because I love you."

"You have a strange way of showing it." Alex took hold of Sue's arms and pushed her away. Feeling the firm flesh between her hands, she said, "You know, you're getting thin."

"Something good's coming out of this then." Sue crossed her arms and let her gaze move down Alex.

Alex laughed. "And what are you going to do? Throw me in the dirty sawdust and ravish me, Miss Butch?"

Sue showed a white-toothed smile, a little startling against her tan. "Want me to?"

Alex's gaze settled on Sue's lower lip. She could almost feel it between her lips, warm and soft. "No. Let's just get this done."

Those Fridays when Ted had Cassie for the weekend, Sue packed in the morning and didn't return to the apartment until Sunday night.

It was as if she had no home, and she wondered if Cassie had felt that way all along, dividing her time as she did between her parents. The apartment seemed almost alien when she returned to it after a weekend at Brenda's — a cold, empty place to endure until once again she could be with Alex. Yet Brenda's trailer never felt like home to her either. She grew tired and restless. Concentration became a slippery thing, hard to maintain.

IX

Once school started, Alex had little time to herself. Preparing lectures and tests, grading exams and reading student papers filled her spare time. Her one free period was taken up with Billy James, who struggled to complete the credits he still needed for graduation. Between classes, other students clamored for her attention.

After school there was volleyball, either practice or a match, then Alex returned to Brenda's to help with the chores and bury herself in schoolwork.

There was a staleness to teaching that had

carried over the summer, a hangover from the letter. She felt differently toward the students, the administration, her fellow teachers. She wondered if her attitude would have been the same had nothing changed, if she were still living with Sue, if the letter had never been written. Thinking about her present situation depressed her.

As she left school Friday evening, hurrying because Sue would be spending the weekend at Brenda's, Lisa Gavinski walked to the parking lot with her.

Lisa hesitated outside Alex's truck as Alex unlocked the door and climbed in. "Sometime I'd like to talk to you. Maybe next week." Lisa smiled, looking as young as a teenager.

"Sure. Next week." Not now, Alex thought. Not even curious, all she wanted to do was hurry the time until she could be alone with Sue.

Janice and Sue drove in one behind the other as Alex changed into jeans and sweatshirt. Looking out the bedroom window, she saw Brenda and Janice walk to the barn and Sue move toward the trailer.

Alex waited, listening to the fast beat of her heart. She heard the front door open and shut, the footsteps coming toward her room.

Sue, her face lighting up, closed the bedroom door behind her. "I hoped you'd be in here."

Alex covered the short distance to Sue in a few strides. Not taking the time to remove any clothing, they fell onto the bed and rushed each other to climax.

"Like we're in heat," Alex said, panting slightly after the exertion, as she belatedly began removing Sue's blouse.

"Yes," Sue agreed, lying prone on the bed, closing her eyes in contentment.

"You have the most beautiful skin," Alex whispered, kissing the golden tan where she had bared it.

Sue opened her eyes and reached for Alex. "Shouldn't we be helping in the barn?"

"Later." Alex's voice was throaty. She buried her face between Sue's breasts with a moan.

Sue shook Alex awake during the night. "Did you hear that?"

"What? What?" Deeply asleep, Alex awakened with difficulty.

Sue hissed, "Shh. Listen."

An insect symphony filled the warm September night. The air vibrated with sound. Alex strained to hear anything unusual over the volume and started to drift back into a somnolent state.

"Hear it? Something's out there." Sue got out of bed and tiptoed to the window, then opened the blinds enough to look outside. The newly installed dusk-to-dawn security light spilled into the room, exposing her nakedness.

Alex joined her at the window. Together they scanned the small yard, the wide dusty barnyard and riding arena. Alex pointed, her voice an explosion of air, "There!"

Although she saw nothing in the shadow of the barn, Sue jumped and squealed. "Should we go out there?" It was the last thing she wanted to do.

Alex started to pull on her clothes. "We better."

Sorry she'd heard anything in the first place, Sue located her clothes in the dark and put them on. "I'll go wake Brenda."

When Brenda didn't answer, Sue opened the door, saw two forms under the sheet and smiled. Good, she thought, and hoped it had been good. "Brenda. We think there's somebody out by the barn."

Brenda leaped out of bed, followed more slowly by Janice. They joined Alex and Sue in the kitchen. "Are you sure someone's out there?" Brenda asked, pulling on a pair of boots.

"I think it might be a good idea to find out. Let's sneak around a little," Alex said. "I'll go with Sue. You and Janice stay together."

"Wait." Brenda reached into a drawer for her revolver and fastened it to her hip.

"Don't shoot us," Sue whispered.

They let themselves out a side door and, bent over in a line, sprinted for cover behind the barn. Brenda and Janice slipped through the rear door of the barn, while Alex and Sue made their way through waist-high weeds to the far end of the building, heading toward the place where Alex thought she had seen movement.

As they rounded the corner of the barn, someone emerged from the shadows and walked quickly toward the road. "Hey," Alex yelled.

The person, too big to be anything but a man, broke into an awkward jog. Alex ran after him, and Sue grasped a handful of Alex's sweatshirt to stop her. "No, Alex."

Sue knew Alex could have caught him; he ran slowly. But what would happen then? Better to let him go. Alex halted, hands on hips, and was joined by the other three women. They watched the figure climb into a large car and drive off.

"Damn it." Brenda stamped a foot. "I don't know where my brains are. I should have gotten the license number at least."

"He wasn't a kid, not one of Billy's friends. He was too big. I wonder what the hell he was doing here?" Alex turned to look at Brenda in the artificial light spilling from the top of the pole near the barn. "Did you find anything in the barn?"

"Not a damn thing. Let's go turn on some lights and look around."

Sue stayed in the parking area, her interest caught by the passenger door of her car. She peered into the Ford, saw only her briefcase. The door was not completely closed, and when she tried it, she found it locked. Puzzled, she stood quietly for a moment, then went to the trailer for her keys. What had he been looking for? What could he want so badly he would sneak around in the night?

Unlocking the car, she searched it methodically and found nothing. It needed a good cleaning, though. Monday or maybe over the weekend, she would take it through the car wash, get it cleaned inside and out.

The other three women emerged from the barn. "Nothing like a good scare to wake you up," Janice remarked, her arms wrapped around herself. "Jesus, I stepped on a cat in the feed room. It let out a screech that curled my hair."

"I heard." Brenda smiled, which was amazing considering someone had been sneaking around her barn. She had probably been thinking arson.

Sue tried to reassure Brenda. "I don't think this had anything to do with the fire."

They all looked at her. "Why don't you?" Brenda asked.

"Like Alex said, he was too big to be one of the suspects. I think he wanted to get into my car." She related her observations.

"Let's go inside." Brenda started toward the trailer with Janice.

"Who was it?" Alex asked, narrowing her eyes and peering intently at Sue in the dim light.

Sue shrugged. "How would I know?" But she lay awake most of the night, certain that she did know. Was she trying to protect him or what, she wondered, watching daylight filter into the room. Exhaustion added weight to her limbs. When Alex stirred and turned toward her, she knew the day had begun.

Sunday night when Sue gathered Cassie from her father's home, Ted opened the door. Friday night seemed a long time gone. She opened her mouth to say something, she wasn't sure what, and Cassie appeared at his side and she said instead, "Hi, honey. Ready to go?" The child disappeared to get her things and Sue told Ted, "I'll call you next week. Okay?"

On the way home she remembered she had forgotten to wash her car. Full of her weekend, Cassie talked nonstop. Suddenly she said, "Daddy's going to buy Shorty, so he'll always be mine. Then we can build a barn to put him in and I can feed him and take care of him."

"Whoa. Back up here. What's that about Daddy buying Shorty?"

"Daddy's gonna talk to Brenda this week." Cassie's face glowed, animated with excitement.

Absentmindedly, Sue had been nudging a lump under the floor mat toward its edge. She leaned down but couldn't quite reach it and still see out the window, so she let it go. Her reaction to Ted's intention to buy Shorty was immediate and intense, but before opening her mouth and voicing it, she decided she had better think about it.

She spent the night considering it, getting very little sleep because it disturbed her so much. She had decided some time ago not to vie with Ted anymore for Cassie's affections. As things stood, she had no chance when it came to purchasing power anyway. Around two in the morning she concluded that her immediate and violent objection came from his attempt to invade her life. Brenda, the barn, riding lessons for Cassie, and Shorty were all part of her world. He had stepped into it without invitation and had started to change it.

"Want to talk after volleyball practice?" Alex asked Lisa Gavinski in the school hall Monday afternoon.

"Sure. I've got enough work here to keep me busy until you're through. But if you don't have time, it's okay."

"I'll make time." Alex continued to the office to

check her mailbox. She joked with the secretaries for a few minutes and waved at Davidson through the door of his office. Then she extracted her mail and looked through it. There was a note from Sue to call her right away. At the pay phone, she dialed Sue's office number.

"Alex, I want you to do something immediately," Sue said. "Promise you won't ask questions and you'll do what I tell you to?"

"What's going on?"

"Promise," Sue insisted.

"Okay. I promise."

"Go to your truck and look under the seats and the floor mats. Look everywhere carefully. Was it locked Friday night?"

"I don't remember. What's wrong?"

"Just do it. And if you find any packages, any little plastic bags, get rid of them. Quickly."

Standing very straight and attentive, Alex listened. "Did you find something in your car?" she asked. Prickles crept up her spine and crawled across her scalp.

"Yes. Under the floor mat. I flushed them down the toilet." There was another pause. "I was stopped by a cop on my way to school. He asked to look in my car."

The goosebumps multiplied and raced over Alex's skin. "The guy out by the barn. Who was it, Sue? Ted?"

"I don't know. Just do it. Now."

"I will. Hang in there, sweetie."

Alex couldn't get to the parking lot fast enough. Under the front seats she found a couple plastic bags — one with a few joints in it, the other containing a small amount of white powder. She crammed them into her pockets and flushed them down the nearest toilet. Only then did she breathe easy.

Why? Who? It preyed on her mind the remainder of the day. Her students somehow knew that she had spun a little out of control, that she wasn't quite in charge, and some tested her. They talked too much and too loud; they interrupted her and their classmates. At last, toward the end of the day, she lost patience with them and raised her voice angrily. "Sit still and be quiet. This isn't open discussion and you aren't the teacher." Then she assigned them two chapters for the next day. When they moaned, she told them not to take advantage. "It'll get you more homework."

After school, she pulled herself together enough to run the volleyball team through routine practice, refining the basics — bump, set, spike, serve.

Alex nearly forgot to look for Lisa Gavinski. She grabbed her briefcase and started to leave the building, then remembered, and went in search of the other teacher.

Lisa looked up from the papers on her desk when Alex entered her classroom. "Can I sit?" Alex motioned toward a chair near the desk.

"Of course." Color started up Lisa's neck until it suffused her unlined face.

Attractive woman, Alex thought, looking at her sister teacher with sympathetic interest in her obvious distress. "What is it, Lisa?"

Lisa shook her head and gave an abrupt laugh. "I can't talk about this. I thought I could but I can't."

Ah ha, Alex thought and took charge of the conversation. "Do you go to the Women's Center often?"

Lisa chewed on her upper lip. Alex could almost see the thought process. "I've been there a few times."

"Sue said she saw you there."

"Alex, I admire you, do you know that?" Alex shook her head and raised her eyebrows and would have asked why, except Lisa continued, "That letter. You remember the letter last spring?"

Alex nodded. How could she forget?

"If that had been directed at me, I would have slunk away somewhere and hid. You took it in stride."

No, she hadn't, Alex wanted to protest and shook her head.

"Well, you continued to teach, to coach. And I thought if you could do that, I should stop pretending, at least to myself." She looked imploringly at Alex.

What did she want? Alex wondered. To confess? To be told it was okay to be herself, whatever that was? "Do you know who wrote that letter? I once thought you might have written it or Mrs. Westover."

The astonished expression on Lisa's face convinced Alex of her innocence. "Why would you think that?" Alex shrugged. "Because I applied for the varsity coaching position?" Alex shrugged again. "Nancy Westover didn't write it either. She didn't like you because of the letter, but she didn't know enough about you to write it. She asked me if it was true."

"What did you tell her?"

"I said I didn't know, but that you were a good coach and teacher."

"Did you?" Alex wondered. Shifting in the hard seat, she leaned forward. "You want to talk about being gay?"

Lisa squirmed uncomfortably. "No. Yes. Sort of."

Suddenly Alex had no patience for word games. "You think you might be gay? It's not so terrible, you know."

"I've only been with men. Once I was even engaged."

"I won't hold that against you." A smile tugged at Alex's mouth. Women, for some reason she didn't understand, often found it necessary to run the gauntlet of male desire. She brushed it aside with a wave of the hand. "You're interested in women?"

"I don't know." Lisa stared fixedly at the papers on her desk.

Alex touched the long slender arm resting on the papers. The other woman appeared vulnerable, confused. "Lisa, it's not a disease or something. It can be wonderful." She thought of Sue and felt a pang. She considered inviting Lisa to the barn but felt strangely reluctant to mix her school and social lives together.

Shocked to see Lisa's blue eyes awash with tears, Alex spoke quietly, "It's okay. I know what it's like to wrestle with being gay."

"It's not okay," the other woman said with vehemence. "My family would disown me."

"You don't have to tell your family. They might not want to know. But, like you said, don't pretend

138

to yourself. Enjoy being a woman loving other women."

"I didn't write that letter, Alex. I would never do that."

"I believe you." And she did.

She drove slowly home from school. She had planned to stop at Billy's but decided against it. The siren startled her. She glanced in the rearview mirror at the flashing lights and pulled over to the side of the road. Rolling down the window, she waited for the police officer to approach.

He looked angry. "You know how long I've been behind you? You should look in your mirror once in a while." He bent and peered in at her.

"Was I speeding?" She had no idea.

"Do you mind stepping out of your truck?"

"If I wasn't breaking any law, why did you stop me?" she asked indignantly, opening the door. What if Sue hadn't called today to warn her? Her next stop might have been jail. Her heart tripped along at high speed. Who? Why? They had better find out.

The officer searched the inside of the truck, then opened the hood and looked carefully under it. He handed her a warrant and told her to empty her pockets, her briefcase, her purse. Alex dumped everything out on the seat and fumed while he fingered through her belongings.

"A bad call, I guess," he said. "You can go now. Sorry."

"Who instigated this?" she demanded.

He shrugged. "I don't know. Call the station."

Better yet, she would go there and protest. Still in furious indignation, Alex confronted a policewoman behind a desk. She got no solid information. The search had been set in motion by an anonymous tip.

Alex stepped into the cool darkness of the barn, her footsteps echoing in the old cement passageways. She poked her head into the tack room, the lounge, the feed room. No one. She could hear voices, though, and followed the sound to the back of the barn where Sue and Janice stood looking toward the large pasture.

The days had shortened. Already the sun hung low in the west. She saw Brenda leading a horse toward the barn. Cassie, clinging bareback to the horse's mane, looked very small. Several horses trailed after them. "Can we talk, Sue?"

They walked toward the lounge. Alex told Sue about the afternoon's events. Then she said, "I think maybe we should have called the police, starting Friday night."

"Probably, but that's hindsight." Sue sighed. "Is he that vengeful? It just doesn't seem Ted-like to be sneaking around in the night. I thought he imagined himself above that sort of behavior."

Alex said, "If Ted did that, he'd do anything."

Sue sighed again and nodded. "I'll talk to him tomorrow."

"You expect him to confess?" Alex asked with feigned astonishment. "Ask him about the letter while you're at it."

The two women stared at each other in silence, each caught up in her own thoughts. Sue probably had difficulty believing Ted would sink that low, but Alex had just about convinced herself that he was responsible for writing the letter and planting the dope and God knew what else. The clip clops of approaching horses broke their concentration. They swung toward the sound.

Cassie bounced on Shorty's back and Brenda said, "Guess what? Someone else wants to buy Shorty. He's in great demand."

"Daddy wants to buy him for me," Cassie put in.

"Oh." Brenda shot a look at Sue. "I didn't catch the last name but the first name was Ted. I just told him Shorty wasn't for sale."

"You can sell him to Daddy. I'll take care of him, Brenda."

"How would I give you lessons then, Cassie? Believe me, it's more fun when you don't have to take care of him all the time."

Cassie slipped off Shorty's back. "You won't sell him ever?"

"Cross my heart," Brenda promised.

While Cassie led the small horse to his stall, Sue thanked Brenda.

"Ted should thank me. Cassie would probably lose interest in taking care of Shorty so fast his head would spin. It's fun here for her with all the activity. It'd be a chore all by herself."

X

Sue called Ted the next day and asked to see him.

"I really don't have time," he said.

"Make time. This is important."

"I can't today. I can't this week. God knows when I'll have time."

"I think I'll have to talk to my dad," she said. He could ignore her. He couldn't overlook her father, who still had a strong voice in the law firm.

He laughed rudely. "Go ahead, run to Daddy. I've got better rapport with your father than you do. I would have to tell him what you and Alex do in your spare time."

"And I'll tell him you were at the barn Friday night and a few other things." She hadn't meant to lay her cards on the table.

He didn't even pause to indicate guilt. "I don't know what you're talking about. I've got to go now. Maybe next week."

"Don't hang up," she said as he did. Goddamn him, she thought, close to tears.

Should she talk to her father? Tell him what she thought was going on? But it was all speculation. She couldn't prove Ted had been at the barn. She wanted to ask Ted face to face, and then in her anger she had blurted out her suspicions. She could have kicked herself. She decided to discuss it with her mother first.

She left Cassie with Brenda and Alex and drove to her parent's condominium that evening. A warm twilight hung over the complex. Streetlamps similar to the gaslights of earlier years cast shadows on the streets and lawns. The buildings all looked alike to her.

Her mother greeted her at the door. Her father sat, as usual, in front of the television with a newspaper to read during commercials. She gave him a kiss on the forehead.

"How's Cassie these days?" he asked without looking at her.

"Good, Dad. How are you?"

"Fine, fine." The short exchange ended.

Sue looked to her mother, who gestured toward the den. Once there, Sue took a deep breath, told herself she had no choice, and handed her mother a copy of the letter. Then she watched Joanne's face, an interesting study in emotions. Sue wanted to laugh hysterically.

"I don't want to read this," Joanne said after the first few sentences. She thrust the letter toward her daughter.

"Read it, Mom. It's important you do."

"Why? I don't want to know about these things. I told you that."

Even now the disapproving expression on her mother's face bothered her. "I think Ted wrote that letter."

"Ted? Why?" Joanne's eyes returned to the paper and she finished reading it, then looked at her daughter. "Who received this?"

Sue told her.

"Alex didn't lose her job, did she?"

"No, but it made everything very difficult for her, even spilled over into her personal life."

Sue explained the man in the barnyard, the dope in both her car and Alex's, Ted's refusal to see her. "First he wanted Alex to lose her job. Now he's trying to destroy our credibility. He probably thinks it'll be easy to get Cassie if we get caught with dope. Maybe he wants us both to lose our jobs. He wants us to be miserable and apart. Who knows?"

Joanne listened, the disapproval on her face turning to doubt. "What do you expect me to do about it?"

"Dad's still got a lot of influence at the law firm. If he'd just talk to Ted, tell him to lay off."

Her mother spoke with disbelief. "I'd have to show your dad this." She rattled the letter. "Do you really want me to do that? He doesn't think you should have left Ted in the first place, and if he knew why ... " She left the sentence unfinished in apparent inability to explain herself.

"I don't know what else to do, Mom. And I didn't leave Ted for Alex or for anyone." She had spent her life trying to please her father, she thought. Fuck it, fuck him.

"Sue, he just might think Cassie would be better off with Ted if he knows about you and Alex."

"He's my father. Doesn't he care about me at all?"

Sitting down with David in a coffee shop booth, Alex ordered Seven-Up. Sue had given him her number at Brenda's. "So, have you talked to Mom and Dad lately?"

David's black hair hung softly over his forehead. "Saturday. They'd like us to make a return visit. Maybe Christmas."

"I know. I don't think I want to go to Florida for Christmas, though. Maybe afterward." She looked into his eyes, so like her own, shaded by long black lashes. "When's your book going to be out?"

"The first of the year."

"I want to buy one of the first copies."

"I'll give you one, autographed." His sudden grin warmed her. "What's happening?"

Once she began, the words rushed out of her non-stop. She told him why she and Sue weren't living together, about the dope planted in their cars. She explained the letter to him for the first time and her most recent suspicions.

"If you could prove he wrote that letter, what would you do about it?"

Having thought this through, she replied immediately. "I'd use it to keep Cassie out of his hands."

Finishing his beer, he ordered another, then said, "What do you need for proof?"

"Something off the same typewriter."

"What if I make an appointment with him? Tell him I want to write an article on him or something. Maybe I can filch something off his desk that'll match the type."

She smiled, wondering why he was willing to do this for her and worried that, if he did, he might get caught. "What if he recognizes the last name or sees the resemblance?"

"The last name will be easy. I'll change it a little. And I'll grow a mustache. I've been wanting to anyway." He met her eyes. "Maybe you should sue him."

"He's an attorney. And everything in the letter is true, except the part about me possibly corrupting students."

Alex saw Billy during her free period. He had discarded his crutches and he limped into her room and plunked himself on a chair near her desk. "You're getting around pretty well, I see," she said with a warm smile. She felt a fondness for Billy she didn't fully understand.

"Yep. My dad says they should have finished the

job, put a few more holes in vital places." He offered her an ironic smile.

Horrified, she only stared.

He spread out a folded piece of paper, smoothed it with one hand, and gave it to her. Then he leaned back in the chair and narrowed his eyes to slits.

The scrawl, difficult to read, was tiny: *I saw the sky, covered with clouds. I felt the pain, burning and intense. Lying face down, pressed against the earth. The cool wet grass, turning red beneath. I suddenly hugged life, held it close.*

She glanced at him, at his burning embarrassed cheeks. She had requested a poem, had gotten this. "This is good, Billy." She read it again. "I'd like to put it in the school paper, if I may."

"You gotta be kidding. I ain't no writer." But she thought he looked pleased.

"You ain't so bad either," she teased him and then grew serious. "The Grand Jury's in session."

"I know." He shifted in his chair.

"You going to tell them what happened?"

"I don't know. They'll kill me for sure, if they think I told on them." It was the most he had revealed to her.

"They almost killed you anyway."

"I think they're gone to Mexico. I can't prove I didn't do it, though."

"I've been summoned," she said.

"I expect so." His wry smile drew his mouth up on one side.

"Well, let's get to work. I love the poem. Why don't you write another for next week?"

He groaned. "It took me a whole night to write that one and it don't even rhyme."

"That's not much time, and poetry doesn't have to rhyme."

Alex testified as did Brenda. Either the jurors believed them or Billy was convincing, because he wasn't indicted. His pale face took on color and he regained some weight. He began stopping by the barn occasionally.

He worked part-time in a welding shop Monday, Tuesday and Wednesday and for a construction firm the other two days. When at the barn, he repaired fences, patched stalls, built corner feeders and jumps, replaced siding and roofing, and performed minor mechanical jobs. Brenda wondered aloud how she had managed without him.

Cassie often dogged his footsteps while he worked. "What are you doing, Billy?" she would ask.

And he would carefully explain, give her tools to hold until he needed them, listen to her chatter and reply gravely when she paused for breath.

David showed up one Sunday afternoon. It had been a quiet day, spent outside doing chores. Autumn touched the warm air, a hint of coolness in the breeze, a few early leaves turning and falling. Expecting him, Alex met him at his Jeep. John got out of the passenger side, and after admiring David's mustache, Sue offered to show John around. It looked a little scraggly, Alex thought, but it definitely changed David's appearance.

When David and Alex were alone, he said, "Ted had some papers typed for me. I picked it up Friday. None of it matches the letter, of course. It was a crazy idea. He's not a stupid man."

"He could have used a typewriter at home."

"Doesn't Cassie ever stay with him?" Alex nodded. "Why don't you ask her to type something when she's there?"

They strolled toward the outside arena where a boarder rode her horse in a cloud of dust. "I hate to use Cassie that way."

"You use what you have to."

Certain Alex would disapprove, Sue had not told her she had shown Joanne the letter. Toward the end of the week Sue wondered whether her mother had ever worked up the courage to talk to her father. Joanne called shortly after Cassie went to bed Sunday night.

"Don't keep me in suspense, Mom. Where's Dad?"

"Asleep. I showed him that letter and he hit the ceiling. He asked me if any of it was true and then went through the roof."

"Sorry, Mom."

"Well, it was better than I thought it would be. After he cooled some, I told him what you told me about Ted."

"Did he talk to Ted?"

"He told Ted that if he planted any of that stuff in your car he'd crucify him and that he'd better think twice about harassing you."

"And what did Ted say?"

Joanne paused. "Ted told your dad he didn't have any right to threaten him. I'm afraid Ted laughed. Your dad was forced to talk to Danson." Danson had become senior partner of the law firm when Sue's father retired.

"And?"

"Ted's on his own."

She couldn't believe it. She hadn't meant for Ted to lose his position with the firm. "You're kidding, Mom."

"I'm not. Mike still has a lot of influence."

"Jesus Christ."

"Must you talk that way?"

Ted called her the next day at school. "Sue, can I see you this week?"

The mountain moves, she thought; it throws up. "When?"

"Whenever. Today for lunch?"

"Okay." Was it her turn to gloat? But it was an unearned victory, soured by the fact that she'd had to use her father to achieve it.

In a booth at the restaurant down the street from Chancelor High, Sue waited for Ted. He strode toward her purposefully, not looking at all chastised. Sliding in across from her, he ordered coffee and a sandwich.

"Your dad did me a favor," he began without greeting.

"How's that?" she asked.

"He got me out on my own where I ought to be."

"Ted, I recognized you sneaking around the barn that Friday night. I know you put dope in my car and Alex's truck, although we didn't keep it long enough to find out what it was. And then you called the cops, hoping we'd get caught with drugs. Our mistake was not to call the police ourselves. We won't make that error again." Talking about it made her more angry than she had been when it happened. Her hands shook, and she hid them in her lap. "I never thought you were such a piece of shit."

"My, my. Potty mouth." He raised his eyebrows.

"You wrote that letter and sent it to Alex's school, too, didn't you?"

"What letter?" A faint smile crossed his lips and was gone.

"Is your life so awful that you can't bear to let me be happy?"

The waitress put their orders in front of them. Sue still didn't trust her hands.

"Even your dad thinks Cassie would be better off with me."

She pulled her dignity around her with difficulty and refused to respond. "Why did you agree to see me? Why did you call?"

"Why not? Oh, I'm going out of town next weekend. I won't be able to take Cassie. Okay if we switch for the next weekend?"

Sue's heart took a dive. Another weekend without Alex in bed. She didn't know if she could bear it.

Sue's reflection in the mirror should have thrilled

her. She had lost weight, almost ten pounds. Her best features, she knew, were her eyes and hair and golden skin — as Alex so often told her.

Cassie approached and stopped by Sue's side. "What are you doing, Mama?"

Sue put an arm around her daughter's shoulders and gazed at her image. "Your mama's getting skinny."

"You look like Mama."

Thinking that she didn't recognize herself anymore, that she needed time away from present circumstances to work some things through in her mind, Sue said, "Would you like to go to Milwaukee to the zoo this coming weekend?"

"Will Alex and Brenda go too?"

"No, I don't think so. Why don't you ask a friend?"

"I'll ask Heather." Cassie frowned around her thumb. Her mother gently removed it from her mouth.

"It's hard to understand you when your mouth's full." They still stood in front of the full-length mirror. Sue regarded her thighs. Were they thinner? "I thought you said she was bossy."

The child looked determined. "I'll be the boss."

"Does there have to be a boss? It's bedtime, sweetie. Why don't you go put your nightie on?"

It was Thursday night and they had just returned from a volleyball game. The Plankton girls ranked first in the conference standings. Cassie was always revved up after a game. "I'm not tired, Mama. I wanna play volleyball and softball when I get big."

"You'll be good too with all this experience. Go

on now, honey." Sue shoved Cassie in the general direction of her bedroom. Picking her bathrobe up off the floor where she had dropped it, she covered herself.

When Sue tucked Cassie into bed, the child asked, "When's Alex coming home?"

Turning as she switched off the light, Sue answered, "I don't know." She had put such thoughts out of her head. Now they returned in a rush.

Climbing into her own bed, she stared at the ceiling. She used to think of herself as decisive. She was not proud of what she had done these past months — none of it. She'd given up Alex rather than fight for Cassie. She'd asked her parents to do her dirty work. She smiled as she imagined her father's reaction to the letter.

She envisioned Alex, her long slender hands. Her own crept between her legs. As she gently stroked herself, her fingers became Alex's and she rose to meet them. It was a distant second from the real thing.

Running through the dark, cool September morning brought no relief to Alex's tortured thoughts.

Brenda had come to her last night to talk, had sat on Alex's bed and struggled to say what was on her mind. "You know, Janice and me, I'm not sure what to do." She looked shamefaced.

Alex laughed a little, she couldn't help it, and Brenda offered her a sheepish grin which made her laugh harder.

"Cut that out," Brenda said, giving Alex a friendly shake.

"I can't." Then, ashamed but unable to stop, she howled with laughter. Tears streamed down her face, her jaws and her stomach ached. She envisioned Brenda and Janice in bed and laughed even harder.

Joining in the laughter, even though it was directed at her, Brenda shook Alex again. Alex pulled her down on the bed, and it happened. The laughter stopped, they stared at each other, and somehow Alex found herself making love to Brenda. Afterward she was appalled.

Now, in the morning light, as her feet scrunched along the berm, she was even more horrified. Brenda had returned to her own bed, shock on her face.

"Sue must never know," Alex had cautioned in a whisper, as if Sue had been there to hear.

"No one must ever know," Brenda had agreed.

Brenda's bathroom door had been open, the room empty, when Alex had let herself out the door half an hour ago. Reluctant to return home, Alex turned onto Smith Road. Pal joined her as she sped past Billy's house. He loped beside her, an escort, until she met the next crossroads where he turned back toward his place.

Hands on hips and huffing into the silent morning, she walked the distance of Brenda's driveway and opened the trailer door. The dishes were still stacked in the sink. Brenda was nowhere to be seen. Now she wanted to see her, to know that she was all right and not devastated by last night. Turning on the shower and stripping off her clothes, Alex stepped under the stream of water. She thought she heard a door open and close, the sound of a radio.

Dressed for school, she walked to the kitchen and surprised Brenda at the sink. "You okay, Brenda?" The big-boned woman flinched and dropped a dish. "I didn't hear you."

"Sorry. I didn't mean to startle you." Alex put a piece of bread in the toaster and leaned against the counter. Feeling awkward, she said, "Want to talk?"

"Can we forget last night?"

"We will. It'll take time is all." Alex smiled a little and couldn't resist asking, "Was it so bad?"

Brenda's face turned crimson, her large features crumpled a little. "No, Alex. That's just it. It was great."

Alex's smile turned into a grin and she clapped Brenda on the shoulder. A mistake. Brenda jumped as if she'd been shot. "Relax, Brenda. You're safe. Consider it a lesson on how it should be done." Dismayed, she listened to her own glib remarks and realized she was very close to laughter again. Was she hysterical or what?

"I just hope you don't think you have to leave because of what happened last night." Brenda wouldn't or couldn't meet Alex's eyes.

Alex took hold of her friend and turned her around. "Where would I go?" She smiled into the stricken eyes. "It was my fault, Brenda. Now I've got to go." She gathered papers for her briefcase and hurried to her truck, forgetting her toast.

The sun, now warm and bright, flooded the Chevy. Rolling down the window and turning up the radio, she tried to dismiss last night from her mind.

But it wouldn't go away easily. She really had been more at fault than Brenda; her inexplicable passion had taken them both by surprise. Grimacing a little, she remembered the response she had elicited from her friend, one of breathless excitement. She had to admit that she had enjoyed sharing her sexual talents with Brenda this one time.

On Friday Sue called Brenda to tell her that she and Cassie would be gone over the weekend. She couldn't understand Brenda's reaction, her uncharacteristic insistence that Sue and Cassie come to the barn. "We're only going to Milwaukee, to the zoo. We're planning to come back. I need to get away, Brenda. I've been doing everything wrong lately."

"Did you ask Alex to go with you?"

"No. I want to do some heavy thinking."

"Why? What is there to think about?" Brenda's alarmed voice filled Sue's ear.

Sue held the phone a few inches away from her head. "Don't shout. What is wrong? I'm only going to be gone a couple days. I want you to tell Alex for me."

"Why don't you tell her?"

"Brenda, calm down. It's hard to reach her. Is something wrong?"

"No, no. Why do you think that? Nothing's wrong."

"You protest too much, woman. You have a good weekend. Give Alex my love."

"You give her your love." Brenda's voice still registered alarm. "But give Cassie mine. Okay?"

"Take it easy, my friend."

"You, too."

Puzzled, Sue stared at the receiver for a few moments as if it could explain Brenda's behavior. Then she shrugged and dismissed it from her mind.

When Sue and Cassie returned to the apartment Sunday afternoon, Sue welcomed even the stale loneliness. She was deeply glad to be home, to feel familiarity take her back in its folds. She willingly replaced escape with routine, welcomed its comforting intimacy. She felt ready to deal with those problems she had sought to shed or solve by putting distance between her and them.

That evening, pulling the blanket to Cassie's chin, she sat quietly on the edge of her bed. "Did you have fun in Milwaukee, sweetie?"

Cassie nodded. "Can I take Heather to the barn next weekend?"

"I guess, if she wants to go. It seems like you two spend a lot of time bragging. I'm not crazy about that, Cassie. Possessions aren't that important."

The girl stared sleepily at her mother as if she either didn't understand or didn't know what to reply.

"Well?"

"She thinks she's got more than me. She says she's got her mama and daddy with her. Why don't you live with Daddy?"

Great, Sue thought wearily. "Daddy and I get along better apart."

"But couldn't we all live in the same house? There's lots of room at Daddy's."

"Honey, Daddy's going to have another wife. You know that."

"But Jean wouldn't mind. I know she wouldn't." Cassie pleaded with her entire body — voice, face, outstretched arms.

"Yes, she would mind, and so would Daddy and I." Horrified at the very thought, Sue attempted to put this insane idea out of her daughter's mind.

"I want Alex to come home," Cassie said in a stubborn tone, crossing her arms and pouting.

"I'm too tired for this tonight, Cassie." Sue bent and kissed her, catching an ear as the child turned away from her. "Sleep tight."

"I won't sleep all night."

But fifteen minutes later, when Sue tiptoed into the room, she found Cassie sleeping soundly — thumb in mouth, an arm outstretched, dark hair covering a rosy cheek, the other against the pillow.

She decided to call Claire D'Aubisson tomorrow and make an appointment. She needed to talk to someone about this displeasure with herself.

Alex had caught Brenda's eye rather often over the weekend, but she hadn't been able to hold it. Brenda's face had reddened and her gaze had slipped away to fasten on some other object. Sunday night, after Janice had gone home, Alex and Brenda sat in the living room.

"Have you thought about asking Janice to move in?" Alex asked.

"I've thought about it, but I'm not sure I want that."

"Would you if I weren't here?"

"You're not fixing to leave, are you?" Brenda frowned at Alex.

"Not yet. I probably should get my own apartment."

"Don't do that, Alex."

"You seem so uncomfortable with me."

"I am right now. I can't help it. But I don't want you to move out. I just want things to be like they were before that happened."

"Sex can spoil a friendship but it doesn't have to."

"What do you think Sue would say if she knew?"

"She'd kill us both."

Brenda looked at her feet propped up on the coffee table in front of her. "I just wish I knew some of what you were doing that night."

"Experiment with yourself." A small smile spread into a big one even as Alex tried to keep it off her face. Brenda turned red, glanced at Alex and then away. "For someone who talks about sex in the animal world without batting an eyelash, I'm surprised you find it so difficult to talk about people."

"It's me I can't talk about. And don't laugh."

"I won't." Alex stood and stretched, the urge to laugh gone. It had been a weekend full of exercise. "I'm going to bed. See you tomorrow."

At school on Monday Billy slouched in a chair near Alex's desk. "Where were you this weekend?" she asked. "We missed you at the barn."

He looked nervously toward the row of windows. "I gotta disappear for a while."

Her heart leaped at his words. "They're back?" Meaning his companions in arson.

He nodded grimly. "They're after me, but it won't hurt you none to keep an eye out."

"Why do you think they're after you?" She studied the steel-gray eyes. Once she had thought them cold, even dangerous. Now she feared for him.

"They must think I talked to the Grand Jury, since I wasn't indicted."

"Did you?"

He shrugged for answer. "I'll watch the barn. I'll be around. Don't worry," he said as if he'd made a decision.

"Can you keep your mind on schoolwork?" She lifted an eyebrow.

"Sure. I been reading like crazy." He grinned and she smiled. "My ma claims it's a miracle because I can't keep my nose out of a book. My old man says only lazy people read."

"And what do you say?" Her smile broadened.

"I got to catch up with all them years I didn't read."

"There's a whole world out there in books. You've just begun to explore it."

"I know and nothing's gonna stop me." He looked determined.

Alex turned cold inside at the thought of what could stop him.

XI

Wondering what to do with the evidence now that she held it, Alex tapped the paper against her hand and stared into space. Looking again at the page Cassie had handed her during regionals, the letters leaped at her from the white sheet.

Alex had asked the child to type her ABCs on her father's typewriter. It would be good practice, she'd said. Like homework.

Now she felt she had pitted the child unwittingly against her father, that she could never use the evidence because of how she had obtained it. The *a* and *g* were identical to those on the letter sent to expose her months ago. There was no doubt that Cassie's practice ABCs and the damaging letter had come off the same typewriter.

With a sigh, Alex set Cassie's page next to the infamous letter on the dresser top, took off her clothes and got into bed. Outside a cold rain pelted the trailer. She stretched full length, hands under her head, and stared into the near dark. The dusk-to-dawn light infiltrated the room even with the blinds closed.

The day had gone well for her. While Sue and Brenda had cheered from the bleachers, her team had won the regionals. Cassie had cleared up the mystery of who wrote the letter, which should have felt like a victory — and might have, had the circumstances been different. She pictured Cassie's bright face glowing with pleasure as she handed Alex the page that implicated Ted.

The opportunity to show Sue the proof of Ted's guilt had not arisen today. Tomorrow, she thought as she slid unresisting into a dream.

The rain ceased to fall toward morning, but Sunday dawned to a cold wind and gray clouds scudding rapidly across a pale blue sky. It felt like November instead of mid-October. Sue shivered as she stepped out of her car at the barn.

Cassie disappeared into the shelter of the barn and Sue, arms wrapped around herself, followed. The dampness inside chilled her nearly as much as the cold wind had. She watched her daughter run ahead, her footsteps echoing.

Cassie paused at the first cross-aisle, looked down it, took a step in that direction. That was all Sue saw, and when she reached the aisle the child had vanished. Sensing something amiss, she stood undecided in the cross-aisle and peered toward where she thought Cassie must be. "Cassie," she called. Then louder, "Cassie." There was no answer and, annoyed, she headed down that passageway. Veering from one side to the other, she peered into the darkened stalls as she walked. Horses nickered at her, poking their soft muzzles through the bars.

She reached the end of the row of stalls that took her to the back aisle of the barn. With no one in sight and no sound to follow, she turned and headed toward the tack room and lounge.

"Hey, Sue. How are you?" Brenda asked. Over Easy, Brenda's seventeen-hand thoroughbred, stood in the cross-ties, dwarfing even Brenda with his height. She tossed a brush toward the tack room, lifted the pad and hunt saddle, and set them on the elegant horse's back. Over Easy swung his long head in Sue's direction and fastened his large brown eyes upon her.

"Have you seen Cassie?" Sue asked, frowning and chewing on her chapped lower lip.

"I was just going to ask you where she was." Both Brenda and the horse stared at Sue.

"She was ahead of me when we came into the barn, then she turned down that first aisle and disappeared. I walked the length of it and didn't hear or see anything."

"Why would she go down that aisle? Shorty's not in that aisle."

"It was like she saw something, but like I said, I didn't see or hear anything."

"Alex is in the house. Tracey's not here and neither are any of the boarders. Who would she see?" Brenda tightened and buckled the girth strap. "Maybe it was Tabby?"

Sue shook her head. "She disappeared then. I looked into all the stalls in that aisle. But they're so dark .. "

"Come on." Brenda put an arm around Sue. "Show me. She can't be far."

They met Alex on their way to where Sue had lost sight of Cassie and Sue had to repeat all she had told Brenda. The three women took different passageways through the barn to search for the girl. They could hear each other's voices calling Cassie's name. Following each call, they listened for some reply but heard only the animals shuffling, chewing, nickering. After they had walked the barn once and met at the tack room, they decided to conduct a more thorough search, one which would take them into each stall, into the feed room, the tack room, the lounge and bathroom. An hour passed before they met again in front of the tack room.

Puzzled, uneasy, they darted worried looks in all directions. Panic touched Sue. She recalled stories of children vanishing like this, never to be seen again.

Alex's eyes showed desperation. "I'm going to get Billy," she said. "I won't be long. You two keep looking."

"Why are you going to Billy's at a time like this?" Sue asked, fright turning to anger.

But Alex was already walking rapidly toward the exit. "I'll be back soon."

Speeding out of the driveway, bouncing off the seat over each rut, Alex's mind raced ahead of her. *They were back,* Billy had said. It was all she could think of — that Cassie had been taken in an attempt to get at Billy. She took the corner at Smith Road on two wheels and burned asphalt for a hundred feet before the truck leveled off. Brakes screaming in protest, she drove onto Billy's yard and shoved the shift stick into neutral. She ran toward the house, Pal joining her on the way, and pounded on the door until Mrs. James opened it. "Billy. I'm looking for Billy," Alex said breathlessly, one hand on Pal's furry head.

"He ain't here." The woman started to close the door.

"Wait." Alex heard a low warning growl from Pal as she pushed the door open. "I've got to find him."

"It's okay, Ma." Billy stepped into view. "You go on. This is Ms. Sundstrum. She's okay." He smiled reassuringly at his mother, who disappeared into the house. Billy tucked a flannel shirt into faded jeans. "What's going on? I told you I had to go into hiding."

This is where he chose to hide? she thought. At his own home? But maybe it was a place no one would look, and Mrs. James would never let on he was here. They'd probably have to torture her to find out Billy's whereabouts. First, though, they'd have to get past Pal.

"Billy, something's happened to Cassie," Alex began.

His response confirmed Alex's fears. He didn't tell her not to worry. His gray eyes only reflected her anxiety. Shutting the door behind him, he stepped out into the cold, windy day as if he felt nothing.

"You need a jacket," she said.

"There's one in my truck. Let's go." His face and mouth looked grim.

"Do you think maybe those guys who set the fire . . ." She couldn't finish the thought.

He shrugged. "They want me. If they got her, they'll let her go for me."

"But they're dangerous."

"So am I right now." He strode around the corner of the house toward the barn.

She followed his old truck as it fishtailed out of the driveway and sped to the barn. She had been gone less than twenty minutes.

Nearly running to keep up with Billy's long stride, Alex trailed him into the depths of the barn where they met Brenda and Sue. There was no need to ask if Cassie had been found. She looked at the fear in their faces and said to Brenda, "Why don't you call the police?"

"No, not yet," Billy said, holding up one hand. "Let me look for her first. You go in the lounge." When the women hesitated, he said, "It's best. Believe me."

"Find her," Alex pleaded.

"Don't worry," he said, his smile not quite reaching his eyes. "Now go on." He herded them into the lounge. "Give me fifteen minutes. Then you can call the police and come out."

The three of them looked at their watches. It was still morning, only ten to twelve, Sue noted with surprise. She and Cassie had arrived at the barn around ten. Not even two hours had passed and it seemed like forever.

Leaning against the door, straining to hear through it, Alex wondered aloud if they were crazy to give this time to Billy. She held Sue close, their hearts beating rapidly.

Unable to bear the confinement, Sue broke free and paced the room, returning every few minutes to stare at the door and at Alex. "Do you hear anything?" she would ask and, when Alex shook her head, resumed her fretful walking.

Brenda, arms crossed and eyes on her friends, rested against the wall next to Alex. She looked coiled and ready to spring into action at any word or sound.

The quiet knock on the door brought them all to attention. Alex spun and opened the door a few inches, then flung it wide. Cassie stood on the other side, her eyes big and frightened. Alex grabbed her and carried her into the room.

Cassie's arms tightened around Alex. Crying, she hid her face in the soft space between the winged collarbone. Wordlessly, Alex handed the child to her mother.

Sue wrapped her arms around her daughter, burying the fingers of one hand in the dark hair. Cassie transferred her grip to her mother, covering her eyes in Sue's neck.

"I'm going for Billy," Alex said. "You stay here, Sue. Lock the door. Brenda, call the police."

"You call the police, Sue. I'm going with Alex," Brenda said.

Before Sue could urge caution, the other two women were gone, and knowing it wouldn't keep anyone out who was determined to get in, she hooked the door behind them. She dialed 911. Cassie clung to her as she gave the dispatcher directions to the barn.

"Mama, Mama, Mama," Cassie said, mouth against her mother's skin.

"It's all right, baby," Sue soothed. "It's okay." Sobs shook the little girl, and her mother wiped away the tears with a paper towel from a roll near the sink. "You're safe, sweetie."

"Where'd Alex and Brenda go?" Cassie tightened her hold until Sue had to pry her loose so that she could breathe.

"They went to find Billy. They'll be all right. Shhh. Don't worry," she murmured, barely able to contain her own worry.

Cassie pushed away from her mother. Dirty streaks lined her cheeks. Her eyes, black pupils dilated, carried a trapped wild look. "Billy. Where's Billy?"

Sue started to set the child on her feet, but

Cassie clung anew and Sue sat down to accommodate her weight. She wondered if anything would ever be the same for Cassie.

"I wanna go home. I wanna go to Daddy's. He won't let anyone take me."

"Honey, I won't let anyone take you."

Noise filtered through the closed door. Someone pounded on it and hollered "Police." Sue went to the door with Cassie still draped around her neck. At the last minute she wondered if it really was the police and hesitated. But she had to trust someone, she decided, and opened the door. Breathing a sigh of relief at the sight of a uniform, she hitched Cassie up in her arms.

"What's going on, ma'am?"

She told him what she knew, which wasn't much. Cassie refused to talk to fill the holes in her story, burying her face in the safety of her mother's body.

The officer told her to lock the door and stay put while he and his partner searched the barn.

Brenda and Alex returned to the lounge with one of the officers who attempted to question Cassie as she sat on her mother's lap. The girl's gaze flitted from face to face, but the panic that had been in her eyes was gone. "You want to tell me what happened," he asked the child.

The room became silent as everyone watched her. "I tried to call Mama. We were in with Dandy, but the man's hand was over my mouth. I couldn't hardly breathe." Cassie leaned back and Sue protectively pulled the child closer.

Sue saw Alex and Brenda exchange looks. Dandy's stall was the first one in the aisle where Cassie had disappeared.

"I looked in the stalls," Sue said. "We all did."

"He carried me up where the hay is," Cassie said.

Again Alex met Brenda's glance. "I think we need to look in the loft." She took a step toward the door.

"You stay here," the other policeman ordered. "I'll go."

"You might need help," Brenda said.

"Not from you two. If I need help, I'll call for it."

The man who had been asking Cassie questions said, "I'll go with you, George," then followed his partner out of the lounge. He told them to call for back-up.

They heard the police sirens about the time they noticed the smoke. "Do you smell it?" Brenda asked, sniffing. "Fire! Alex, come on."

"Take Cassie and get the hell out of here," Alex said to Sue.

"Be careful, both of you," Sue called to their retreating backs. Feeling she had no choice because she couldn't leave Cassie to go with them, Sue carried her daughter out of the barn. The sounds of frightened animals filled her ears as she hurried away from the building. When she stood in the barnyard to look, she saw fire shooting out of the hayloft.

"The horses'll burn, Mama," Cassie screamed in Sue's ear.

Helpless to leave her daughter, Sue could only watch the flames reach for the roof. The sirens of the approaching fire trucks pierced the air but didn't quite drown out the crackling of the blaze.

Alex and Brenda raced from stall to stall, opening doors, herding horses toward the back door and pasture. Whipping the animals to get them moving, dodging their panicked feet, wasting valuable time forcing horses away from their stalls where they sought safety, Brenda and Alex worked against time. The frantic animals whinnied in fright, spun in the narrow smoke-filled aisles.

Alex shouted and heard Brenda shouting, "Out, goddamn it, get out!"

The animals thundered down the narrow passageways, following each other in mindless panic. Some managed to slip back into the stalls. Alex heard a scream behind her and sped toward the sound. A burning beam had fallen in one stall and a horse was spinning in front of it. She entered the ten-by-twelve area and forced the animal out into the aisle, then slammed the stall door so he couldn't reenter. "Go on, git." When she wielded her whip at his front legs, the terrified animal whirled and kicked. Ready for this, she dodged and laid the whip on his backside. The horse lunged away from her.

Timbered beams fell behind them and flames gobbled the creosoted stall boards. Alex and Brenda stood in the back doorway momentarily unable to take their eyes off the fire consuming the wood with a voracious appetite. Finally, coughing, they stumbled out of the barn.

Doubled over with hands on knees, gasping for breath through what felt like singed lungs, they stared at the burning building.

"Come on, Brenda," Alex said when she no longer struggled for air. "Sue'll be frantic."

"You go. I'll check the horses. They need calming." Her face soot-blackened, Brenda took a step, teetered and fell forward with a sharp cry. Her hands clutched her thigh.

"What is it, Brenda?" Alex bent over her friend, touched the leg. The jeans covering it felt warm, sticky, wet. Alex looked at her fingers. "Are you bleeding?"

"I got kicked."

"Let me get you up and out of here." Smoke hung over them, rolled away with the wind. The intense heat emanating from the old barn burned Alex's face. She helped Brenda to her feet. "Put your arm over my shoulders. We'll walk together."

They hobbled around the perimeter of the barn, somehow managed to climb a fence, and slowly reached the barnyard where three fire trucks, hoses spraying and lights flashing, were parked. Three police cars, lights also turning, blocked the driveway from the curious. Uniformed figures scurried everywhere. Alex looked at the sky, surprised to see daylight.

With Cassie in tow, Sue had been pacing. Time had spun endlessly for her. Unable to leave her terrified daughter with strangers, she had urged the firemen to look for Alex and Brenda. A few had entered the smoke-filled interior, but the intensity of the fire had forced them back outside. Sniffling, Sue let her tears run unchecked.

Cassie spied Alex and Brenda first and, releasing her hold on her mother, she ran to them. Throwing herself against Alex's legs, she hugged her thighs. Alex smiled sadly.

Sue approached them. She said in a quiet, relieved voice, "I was so afraid." Reaching toward Alex with both hands, she touched her blackened cheeks, came away with sooty palms. "Are you all right?" she asked in a shaky voice.

Alex nodded. "I'm okay, but Brenda needs help. She got kicked."

"I'll be fine," Brenda protested. And later, even as she was loaded into a waiting ambulance, she said, "I'm not going."

"Yes, you are," Sue replied firmly.

"Someone's got to see to the horses."

"Sue and I will," Alex reassured her.

The ambulance, lights circling, pulled around the police barriers and bounced slowly down the rutted driveway.

Alex, Sue and Cassie turned their attention to the fire. The barn roof collapsed while they watched, and the walls caved in shortly thereafter. The gallons of water cascading on the burning structure only slowed the process of consumption by fire. The old building burned to the ground and even the dirt turned to fire. Years of hay and straw and sawdust and dried wood offered ample food to the flames.

"Billy?" Alex asked in a quiet voice.

Sue shook her head helplessly and glanced at Cassie, who stood between them. Their arms crossed behind the child's back and held her shoulders.

"Could he have been in the loft?" Alex's sooty face looked eerie in the glow cast by the leaping flames.

Sue grimaced. "I hope not." She asked about the horses. "Did you get them all out?" She looked at Alex and recalled that less than an hour ago she had been begging God, whom she had given up believing in years ago, for Alex's safety. She had felt immense gratitude when Alex and Brenda had turned up safe.

"I don't know. We did our best." Alex shuddered, exhaustion and pain playing across her face.

"Mama, where's Tabby?" Cassie asked loudly, alarmed.

Sue glanced at Alex, who shrugged. "We'll look soon."

Alex left to find out about Billy. When she returned, she repeated the policeman's words: There had been no one in the barn. Then she said wearily, "I should go back to the pasture and check the horses. Some may need a vet." She looked around the barnyard, noticing a few familiar faces who might help.

Sue's mother joined them. Sue was so surprised to see her that she only stared and asked without preamble, "What are you doing here, Mom?"

"I heard about the fire on the radio." Joanne took Cassie in her arms, held her granddaughter close and crooned to her. Then she spoke to Sue. "I'll take Cassie home with me. Wouldn't that be best?"

"That'd be wonderful, Mom. I'll call you later."
Sue hugged them both and gratefully relinquished
the child's care to Joanne.

Some of the boarders, Tracey the barn girl, and
the barn's two veterinarians showed their concern for
the animals by their presence. They had convinced
the police of their right and need to be at the scene.
Now they went with Alex and Sue to check on the
animals.

They found the horses huddled at the far end of
the pasture. A few of these helpers had brought
halters and lead ropes. Skittish and milling around,
the animals proved difficult to catch and treat. The
veterinarians administered tranquilizers, sprayed
medication on abrasions, and stitched and bandaged
the more serious wounds.

Then came the problem of feed. Fortunately, the
water tanks had been filled the previous day.
Neighboring farmers stood ready to donate hay and
grain until Brenda could supply her own.

Alex had been counting heads. Shorty and Satan
and Over Easy were among the rescued horses. She
knew that some animals were missing and assumed
they had died in the fire. She tried to recall the
identities of the absent horses and couldn't.

Tired beyond belief, Alex could hardly believe the
sun hadn't set, although it hung low and yellow in
the western sky.

When there was only one fire truck left to tend
to the smoldering ruins and two policemen to turn

away the curious public, Sue urged, "Let's go inside." She smiled a little, as if grateful they had survived the day.

Surveying her surroundings, Alex stood with hands on hips. Turning toward Sue, she asked, "Will you stay the night?"

"You couldn't beat me away," Sue replied.

"I've done all the beating I want to do in my lifetime," Alex remarked, remembering the horses.

As they entered the trailer, the cats appeared from underneath it. One by one they clustered at the door. She greeted them, investigating each one for damage and finding none. She put water and food outside. They had already found shelter.

XII

Flames burned behind Alex's eyelids all night, but she did not awaken until early morning. An exhausted sleep had claimed both women when they went to bed shortly after dark Sunday night. They had not eaten since breakfast the previous day and when Alex opened her eyes to the sound of icy rain, she felt hunger. Working deeper under the blankets, she hated to leave the warm bed.

"You awake?" Sue asked sleepily.

"I'm starving. I don't think I ate all day yesterday. Want to see what's in the fridge?"

"It sounds cold out there. That's what we needed yesterday. Rain."

But they didn't get up. Instead, they slipped back into slumber, and the fire burned once more in Alex's dreams.

The necessity of providing shelter for the animals kept Alex and Sue occupied all morning. Via the phone they farmed the horses out with neighbors until their owners or Brenda could decide what to do with them. Then the two women hand-delivered them to their temporary shelters, leading the shivering, sodden beasts along the roads.

Late in the afternoon they took the last three horses — Shorty, Satan and Over Easy — to Michelle's small barn. Cold and wet even in slickers, they accepted Michelle's offer of a ride home if she would first take them to Billy's.

As she parked in Billy's driveway, Michelle asked, "Want me to go to the door? I know the dog." The house looked uncared for and deserted.

"Alex knows him pretty well too," Sue said, as Alex stepped out and stooped to pat Pal.

Alex walked with him to the front door and pounded on it, waited as she listened for footsteps inside, then banged more insistently. Pressing her ear to the wood, she thought she heard someone approaching. Minutes passed. Teeth chattering, she shivered in her rain-soaked jeans and tennis shoes. Pal leaned against her leg, warming it with his body heat, and she worried about him in the cold, soaking rain. Where did he find shelter? In the barn behind the house? No one answered her summons. She turned away from the unyielding house and, tucking her head against the wet wind, hurried to the dry warmth of the car.

"Let me know if you see or hear from Billy, Michelle," Alex said when the girl dropped them at the trailer. "And thanks for the ride."

They phoned the hospital while getting out of their cold, stiff clothes. Alex talked to Brenda.

"I've been calling everywhere," she protested. "Neither of you went to school? Come rescue me, please."

"We didn't think you'd be able to go home so soon."

"It can't be soon enough for me. Bring me some sweats, big ones. Okay? I can't get this cast into a pair of jeans." Brenda had suffered a line fracture.

"I better call my mother," Sue said after Alex hung up. They'd agreed to leave Cassie with her parents another day at least.

"How is she, Mom?" Sue thought of the night of dreams spent looking for her daughter and never finding her. As she talked, she absently read the letters on the dresser in Alex's room.

Cassie was doing well, Joanne told Sue, and of course she could stay another day or two. They would love to have her.

"What is this, Alex?" Sue asked, holding Cassie's typewritten page in her hand. When Alex told her, she could only say, "I'm sorry." She wished it hadn't been Ted who had done this terrible thing to Alex because it made her feel nearly as culpable, certainly responsible. She had shown herself a poor judge of character when she had married him.

Alex's hair curled wetly around her face, and her thick, glistening lashes dripped moisture. Dressed only in a sweatshirt and panties, she leaned one hand against the dresser. "You don't need to apologize," she said. "I feel terrible that I asked Cassie to type that for me. I don't think I can ever use it."

Gently cupping Alex's chin with one hand, Sue spoke her mind. "I should never have asked you to leave, Alex. Will you come back?"

Staring at Sue in surprise, Alex kissed the hand holding her chin. "What about Cassie?"

"I'll fight for her. It's what I should have done in the first place."

"And if you lose? I don't want to be responsible for that."

"I don't think I'll lose." Sue moved a step closer to Alex. "I'm not going to let Ted decide my life for me anymore."

"I can't leave Brenda now. She'll need help." Alex took hold of Sue's shoulders. Running her hands down Sue's arms to her hips, she pulled her close.

Sue slid her arms around Alex's waist. "We won't leave her. We can stay here, can't we, until she's on her feet again? There's room for all of us."

That night over dinner, Alex asked, "Did you have the barn insured for enough, Brenda?" She was thinking that winter was on its way and all those horses needed shelter.

Brenda shrugged listlessly. "Enough to build a small barn, just for my stock. I'll go work in the mill again. I'm not going to be responsible for anyone else's animals." She caught her breath and asked the question that must have haunted her. "How many got out?"

"I'll show you the list in a minute. Just listen now. Neighbors have been calling. They want to help rebuild the barn."

"Billy, too, I suppose," Brenda said with a tight smile. The other two exchanged looks while she watched them. "Why is his truck still here?"

Alex studied her food. She envisioned Billy throwing a softball and her vision blurred.

Brenda turned to Sue. "Where is Billy?"

Swallowing, Sue said, "We don't know."

Brenda's voice rose. "He didn't get out of the barn?"

"The police think there was no one in the barn."

Brenda stared at them. "That's it. I'm getting out of this business. Billy. The horses. I feel like a goddamn murderer." She crossed her arms as if to brook no objections. "Where's Cassie?"

"At my mother's." Sue glanced at Alex. "I want to stay here with you and Alex. I don't want to leave her again."

"Well, that's good news," Brenda said and burst into tears. Her shoulders shook and she waved away any comfort. "Just get me a box of tissues. Did something good come out of this then?"

"It gave me the push I needed. I was getting there. I talked to D'Aubisson about it."

"Look, if Alex wants to move back to the apartment, that's okay. I can get along."

"We'll stay here, if it's all right with you," Alex said.

"I'm going to call the boarders and tell them to make other arrangements. Would you get me the portable phone?" Brenda gestured at the cast holding her down.

"No. I want you to give it till the end of the week," Alex said. The end of the week would be sectionals. Why did all this have to happen now?

"I won't change my mind, but I'll wait a couple days. I don't really want to talk to anyone else anyway."

"How about Janice?" Sue asked. "Do you want to talk to her?"

Brenda's face lit up with pleasure. She sniffed and actually smiled.

Quickly adapting to crutches, Brenda hobbled around the trailer over the course of the evening. She sent Sue and Alex to bed with a few curt words: "Leave me be. Okay? It hurts and I've got a lot on my mind." When they offered to stay up with her, she shook her head. "I want to be alone."

The arson squad showed up Tuesday as Sue and Alex left for work. Their van drove in and parked near the fallen barn. Armed with equipment, three men got out. Alex did not envy them their task. The sun, a faint light behind gray clouds, offered little heat. Brisk wind sent dead leaves scurrying over yellow grass. Dust rose and swirled across the barnyard. There was nothing redeeming about the morning.

A long five days stretched ahead for Alex: classes, practice, then sectionals on the weekend. She had slept dreamlessly, dead-tired, the past two nights.

Curled against Sue, one arm tucked around the soft curves, face in the thick fresh-smelling hair, she felt somewhat renewed in the mornings.

Billy, she thought. Where the hell was he? She hoped desperately they wouldn't find him in the ashes. He had come such a long way. To end up dead would be too much tragedy. But if he wasn't dead, he had to be with his arson-prone companions. They would probably kill him to quiet him. Recalling his touching poem, she silently pleaded that he not be lying on the grass somewhere shot through with bullets.

Parking next to Lisa's car, she walked into school with her. Lisa was all questions about the fire, and Alex gave her short answers.

"Would you like me to take practice tonight?" Lisa offered.

Alex smiled. "That would be great. Thanks."

Sue called her mother from school that morning. "I'll pick Cassie up tonight. We'll be staying at Brenda's for a while, probably until she's able to walk again." Sue paused and stacked paper clips. "I'll let you know when the three of us move back to the apartment."

Her mother caught the drift quickly. "Alex is moving back, too?"

"Yes. I'm not going to let Ted tell me how to live my life, Mom." She tried very hard not to sound defensive.

Her mother sighed. "All right, dear."

Then she called Brenda, who said, "You and

Alex, all you do is worry. She just called me. Everyone's calling and coming over. There's no rest." But she sounded rather pleased.

"Who's everyone?" Sue rocked back in her desk chair and tucked the phone under her chin.

"Boarders. Neighbors. Some have even come over. They brought food. We have enough food here to feed us the rest of the week." Brenda paused. "They offered to help build a new barn."

Brenda must be reconsidering, Sue thought. "And?"

"I talked to a couple boarders. They still want me to keep their horses. One person called who lost one of her horses in the fire." Brenda's voice quavered. "She wants me to board the other horse."

"You all right?"

"I'll be okay as long as they don't find Billy out there."

"You haven't been outside, have you?"

"I'm going. I haven't gotten away from the phone. It's strange not having anything to do."

"You be careful walking around on those crutches."

After school, Sue headed to her parents' condominium. Heat washed over her as her mother waved her through the door with a sweep of her hand. She noticed her father planted, as usual, in his chair. A fire burned behind glass doors in the fireplace, and she winced at the sight of the red and blue flames. She saw Cassie frowning at her from the doorway to the kitchen.

Sue dropped the obligatory kiss on her father's forehead. She thought he flinched at her touch. "Thanks for keeping Cassie," she said, knowing the effort of caring for their granddaughter had fallen not on him but on Joanne.

"She's a good little girl," he said gruffly.

Sue glanced at Cassie who remained silent. She supposed the child felt abandoned at a difficult time. "Hi, honey. Ready to go to Brenda's?"

Once they were in the car, Sue said, "I had to let Grandma take you. There was too much that had to be done. You were safer and better off with Grandma and Grandpa."

Cassie settled back in her seat and asked, "How's Brenda?"

"Her leg's in a cast, but she's home. Alex and I are taking care of her."

"How's Billy?"

"I'm sure he's fine," she lied, hoping it was true. Realizing that Cassie had forgiven her, Sue squeezed her daughter's leg, evoking a smile.

The trailer, once large and empty with only Brenda as occupant, had become a noisy place. Doors slammed, voices filled every room. At suppertime the table was crowded with people and food. Janice often stayed over, Alex shared her bed with Sue, Cassie spent the nights alone in the small third bedroom.

The child loved it. The cats under the trailer. All the people in it. She blossomed with the attention, even though she stood at the bottom of the pecking order with everyone her boss. Her school papers adorned the refrigerator. She herself accounted for much of the noise. She hated leaving — for school or for weekends with her father.

The day Ted remarried, Cassie participated in the wedding. Sue picked her up after the reception. The child wore a long, simple pink dress with pink shoes and flowers in her hair. Her eyes still reflected the excitement, and food stained her rosy mouth and cheeks. Sue asked, "How was Daddy's wedding?"

"I walked down the aisle and everyone stood up and watched. It was more fun afterwards at the party. Now I don't have to go to Daddy's for a long time — two weeks. He and Jean are going on a honeymoon."

"Isn't that nice?" Sue said wryly.

"Don't get married, Mama."

Smiling broadly, Sue patted her daughter's leg. "You don't have to worry about that, sweetie."

The new barn rose toward the sky ragged with windblown clouds. It would be an L-shaped structure, the long end made to house two rows of back-to-back stalls, a tack room, grooming area, and lounge with bathroom; the short end of the L would be an indoor arena. Brenda showed guarded excitement over the construction.

The rapidity with which the building grew each day startled Alex. Sectionals were over — her team had lost a heartbreaker. In a way she had been relieved that she wouldn't be distracted by continued practice for state competition. Her players had cried over the loss, and she had praised them for their efforts and their sportsmanship. She thought how every phase of her life had been put in perspective:

first by the letter, then by her separation from Sue, and lastly by the barn fire. Crying should be reserved for serious occasions, she thought, and going to state was not one of them.

Billy was one of them. It had been three weeks since his disappearance. She had been to his house numerous times and finally spoken with his mother. She had peered suspiciously at Alex through the partially open door. Mrs. James claimed she had not heard from her son and asked Alex where he had gone.

His remains had not been found in the ashes of the barn. The bones of four horses had been recovered. They must have returned to their stalls and refused to leave. She wondered if she would ever get their screams out of her head. At night she sometimes woke up drenched in sweat from dreams she could not recall. She asked Brenda if she dreamed about the fire when they were standing inside the framework of the new barn.

Brenda leaned on her crutches and looked up at the gray sky. Snow was forecast. She said she thought she would never feel truly secure again. "When the house and garage burned, I thought the worst had happened. You don't expect horrible things to happen to yourself. You know? Now I realize they do." She smiled grimly at Alex. "I dreamed constantly the first week, mostly that I was in the fire again and my leg was broken. I couldn't get out and I couldn't get any of the horses out either."

Alex said, "I never remember my dreams. Maybe that's best." She hugged her jacket closer. Night fell early.

Looking at Alex, Brenda spoke hesitantly. "You know what, though? I was thinking about this today. I'm not afraid to try anything anymore."

Smiling at her friend, Alex understood. Brenda's greatest fear had been personal intimacy. "Life's too iffy to take it for granted, isn't it? That last fire just sort of gave everything a sense of proportion."

December again. The outward structure of the barn stood complete, red galvanized steel outer walls with a white roof. A third of the stalls were constructed and already housed horses. Everyone worked to finish the remaining stalls, aiming to have the rest of the horses in the new barn by Christmas.

Brenda had asked Sue and Alex to move in permanently with her. "Why keep that apartment when you're never there?"

"Have you asked Janice, too?" Sue suggested. After all, Janice spent most of her nights with Brenda anyway.

"I have asked her, but I could use you two here — that is, if you want to stay. Janice knows nothing about horses."

Alex and Sue agreed to discuss it. They had yet to return to the apartment. But sometimes, they both thought, it would be nice to be alone — especially when Cassie was at Ted's.

"She does need us, though," Alex said as they lay together in bed. Snow beat against the window, radiating cold through the glass.

"I know." Sue lay with her head on Alex's shoulder, idly stroking her lover. They had been talking about Brenda's proposition for days now.

"Why don't we do it and then start looking for a house of our own. We'll probably find something before spring. By then Brenda should be able to manage on her own."

A week before Christmas the stalls were finished and filled with horses. The new barn smelled strongly of treated oak and pine. It had wide aisles and skylights and windows that would open out. The loft covered the entire stall area, the lounge and tack room. Large doors hung on the west and east ends of the building to allow fresh air through the aisles. Sawdust bedded the stalls and five inches of sand covered the length and breadth of the riding arena. The new barn had none of the appeal of the old, none of the mystery. But both Alex and Brenda admitted it was easier to work in the new building, since it had been planned to accommodate horses rather than converted to that purpose.

Three days before Christmas, Cassie ran to the feed room for some food supplements Alex had forgotten. Unable to find them, she called Alex and they sought out Brenda in the lounge. Together they saw Billy on the news. The three of them stared at the television set as the reporter droned on about how Billy James had been found with two other young men. All had been charged with setting two serious fires.

They waited up that night for the ten o'clock news. Snow blanketed the ground. Wind rocked the trailer. Billy was the lead story on the regional news.

Jumping up and down with excitement, Cassie

pointed at the television. "Why's he got those handcups on his arms? He didn't do anything."

"Handcuffs," Sue quietly corrected.

"Are they gonna put him in jail?" Cassie continued.

"No, we won't let that happen," Brenda promised from the couch where Janice sat close to her.

"He's alive," Alex said more to herself than anyone else. Relief poured through her, giving her strength. She met Sue's eyes, and they exchanged a smile that grew until they were grinning foolishly at each other.

Since the fire their lovemaking had been tinged with despair, as if they shouldn't be enjoying each other in the midst of death and Billy's disappearance.

When everyone had gone to bed, they huddled together under the blankets in the coolness of their room, burrowing deeper into the bed until they were both thoroughly warmed.

"Let's celebrate," Alex murmured, seeking Sue's mouth with her own.

"We'll be tired tomorrow."

"Do you care?"

"No. I feel like we're starting fresh."

Alex thought briefly of her infidelity with Brenda, then put it aside as she felt Sue's hands on her. And even as their passion grew, a feeling of peace settled over them.

A few of the publications of
THE NAIAD PRESS, INC.
P.O. Box 10543 • Tallahassee, Florida 32302
Phone (904) 539-5965
Mail orders welcome. Please include 15% postage.

STICKS AND STONES by Jackie Calhoun. 208 pp. Contemporary
lesbian lives and loves.   ISBN 1-56280-020-5   9.95

DELIA IRONFOOT by Jeane Harris. 192 pp. Adventure for Delia
and Beth in the Utah mountains.   ISBN 1-56280-014-0   9.95

UNDER THE SOUTHERN CROSS by Claire McNab. 192 pp.
Romantic nights Down Under.   ISBN 1-56280-011-6   9.95

RIVERFINGER WOMEN by Elana Nachman/Dykewomon.
208 pp. Classic Lesbian/feminist novel.   ISBN 1-56280-013-2   8.95

A CERTAIN DISCONTENT by Cleve Boutell. 240 pp. A unique
coterie of women.   ISBN 1-56280-009-4   9.95

GRASSY FLATS by Penny Hayes. 256 pp. Lesbian romance in
the '30s.   ISBN 1-56280-010-8   9.95

A SINGULAR SPY by Amanda K. Williams. 192 pp. 3rd spy novel
featuring Lesbian agent Madison McGuire.   ISBN 1-56280-008-6   8.95

THE END OF APRIL by Penny Sumner. 240 pp. A Victoria Cross
Mystery. First in a series.   ISBN 1-56280-007-8   8.95

A FLIGHT OF ANGELS by Sarah Aldridge. 240 pp. Romance set at
the National Gallery of Art   ISBN 1-56280-001-9   9.95

HOUSTON TOWN by Deborah Powell. 208 pp. A Hollis Carpenter
mystery. Second in a series.   ISBN 1-56280-006-X   8.95

KISS AND TELL by Robbi Sommers. 192 pp. Scorching stories by
the author of *Pleasures*.   ISBN 1-56280-005-1   8.95

STILL WATERS by Pat Welch. 208 pp. Second in the Helen
Black mystery series.   ISBN 0-941483-97-5   8.95

MURDER IS GERMANE by Karen Saum. 224 pp. The 2nd
Brigid Donovan mystery.   ISBN 0-941483-98-3   8.95

TO LOVE AGAIN by Evelyn Kennedy. 208 pp. Wildly
romantic love story.   ISBN 0-941483-85-1   9.95

IN THE GAME by Nikki Baker. 192 pp. A Virginia Kelly
mystery. First in a series.   ISBN 01-56280-004-3   8.95

AVALON by Mary Jane Jones. 256 pp. A Lesbian Arthurian
romance.   ISBN 0-941483-96-7   9.95

STRANDED by Camarin Grae. 320 pp. Entertaining, riveting
adventure.   ISBN 0-941483-99-1   9.95

THE DAUGHTERS OF ARTEMIS by Lauren Wright Douglas.
240 pp. Third Caitlin Reece mystery.   ISBN 0-941483-95-9   8.95

CLEARWATER by Catherine Ennis. 176 pp. Romantic secrets
of a small Louisiana town.   ISBN 0-941483-65-7   8.95

THE HALLELUJAH MURDERS by Dorothy Tell. 176 pp.
Second Poppy Dillworth mystery.   ISBN 0-941483-88-6   8.95

ZETA BASE by Judith Alguire. 208 pp. Lesbian triangle
on a future Earth.   ISBN 0-941483-94-0   9.95

SECOND CHANCE by Jackie Calhoun. 256 pp. Contemporary
Lesbian lives and loves.   ISBN 0-941483-93-2   9.95

MURDER BY TRADITION by Katherine V. Forrest. 288 pp.
A Kate Delafield Mystery. 4th in a series. ISBN 0-941483-89-4   18.95

BENEDICTION by Diane Salvatore. 272 pp. Striking,
contemporary romantic novel.   ISBN 0-941483-90-8   9.95

CALLING RAIN by Karen Marie Christa Minns. 240 pp.
Spellbinding, erotic love story   ISBN 0-941483-87-8   9.95

BLACK IRIS by Jeane Harris. 192 pp. Caroline's hidden past . . .
                                          ISBN 0-941483-68-1   8.95

TOUCHWOOD by Karin Kallmaker. 240 pp. Loving, May/
December romance.   ISBN 0-941483-76-2   8.95

BAYOU CITY SECRETS by Deborah Powell. 224 pp. A Hollis
Carpenter mystery. First in a series.   ISBN 0-941483-91-6   8.95

COP OUT by Claire McNab. 208 pp. 4th Det. Insp. Carol Ashton
mystery.   ISBN 0-941483-84-3   9.95

LODESTAR by Phyllis Horn. 224 pp. Romantic, fast-moving
adventure.   ISBN 0-941483-83-5   8.95

THE BEVERLY MALIBU by Katherine V. Forrest. 288 pp. A
Kate Delafield Mystery. 3rd in a series. (HC) ISBN 0-941483-47-9 16.95
                          Paperback   ISBN 0-941483-48-7   9.95

THAT OLD STUDEBAKER by Lee Lynch. 272 pp. Andy's affair
with Regina and her attachment to her beloved car.
                                          ISBN 0-941483-82-7   9.95

PASSION'S LEGACY by Lori Paige. 224 pp. Sarah is swept into
the arms of Augusta Pym in this delightful historical romance.
                                          ISBN 0-941483-81-9   8.95

THE PROVIDENCE FILE by Amanda Kyle Williams. 256 pp.
Second espionage thriller featuring lesbian agent Madison McGuire
                                          ISBN 0-941483-92-4   8.95

I LEFT MY HEART by Jaye Maiman. 320 pp. A Robin Miller
Mystery. First in a series.   ISBN 0-941483-72-X   9.95

THE PRICE OF SALT by Patricia Highsmith (writing as Claire
Morgan). 288 pp. Classic lesbian novel, first issued in 1952 . . .
acknowledged by its author under her own, very famous, name.
                                        ISBN 1-56280-003-5   8.95

SIDE BY SIDE by Isabel Miller. 256 pp. From beloved author of
Patience and Sarah.   ISBN 0-941483-77-0   8.95

SOUTHBOUND by Sheila Ortiz Taylor. 240 pp. Hilarious sequel
to *Faultline.*   ISBN 0-941483-78-9   8.95

STAYING POWER: LONG TERM LESBIAN COUPLES
by Susan E. Johnson. 352 pp. Joys of coupledom.
                                        ISBN 0-941-483-75-4   12.95

SLICK by Camarin Grae. 304 pp. Exotic, erotic adventure.
                                        ISBN 0-941483-74-6   9.95

NINTH LIFE by Lauren Wright Douglas. 256 pp. A Caitlin
Reece mystery. 2nd in a series.   ISBN 0-941483-50-9   8.95

PLAYERS by Robbi Sommers. 192 pp. Sizzling, erotic novel.
                                        ISBN 0-941483-73-8   8.95

MURDER AT RED ROOK RANCH by Dorothy Tell. 224 pp.
First Poppy Dillworth adventure.   ISBN 0-941483-80-0   8.95

LESBIAN SURVIVAL MANUAL by Rhonda Dicksion.
112 pp. Cartoons!   ISBN 0-941483-71-1   8.95

A ROOM FULL OF WOMEN by Elisabeth Nonas. 256 pp.
Contemporary Lesbian lives.   ISBN 0-941483-69-X   8.95

MURDER IS RELATIVE by Karen Saum. 256 pp. The first
Brigid Donovan mystery.   ISBN 0-941483-70-3   8.95

PRIORITIES by Lynda Lyons 288 pp. Science fiction with
a twist.   ISBN 0-941483-66-5   8.95

THEME FOR DIVERSE INSTRUMENTS by Jane Rule. 208
pp. Powerful romantic lesbian stories. ISBN 0-941483-63-0   8.95

LESBIAN QUERIES by Hertz & Ertman. 112 pp. The questions
you were too embarrassed to ask.   ISBN 0-941483-67-3   8.95

CLUB 12 by Amanda Kyle Williams. 288 pp. Espionage thriller
featuring a lesbian agent!   ISBN 0-941483-64-9   8.95

DEATH DOWN UNDER by Claire McNab. 240 pp. 3rd Det.
Insp. Carol Ashton mystery.   ISBN 0-941483-39-8   9.95

MONTANA FEATHERS by Penny Hayes. 256 pp. Vivian and
Elizabeth find love in frontier Montana. ISBN 0-941483-61-4   8.95

CHESAPEAKE PROJECT by Phyllis Horn. 304 pp. Jessie &
Meredith in perilous adventure.   ISBN 0-941483-58-4   8.95

LIFESTYLES by Jackie Calhoun. 224 pp. Contemporary Lesbian
lives and loves.   ISBN 0-941483-57-6   8.95

VIRAGO by Karen Marie Christa Minns. 208 pp. Darsen has
chosen Ginny.   ISBN 0-941483-56-8   8.95

WILDERNESS TREK by Dorothy Tell. 192 pp. Six women on
vacation learning "new" skills.   ISBN 0-941483-60-6   8.95

MURDER BY THE BOOK by Pat Welch. 256 pp. A Helen
Black Mystery. First in a series.   ISBN 0-941483-59-2   8.95

BERRIGAN by Vicki P. McConnell. 176 pp. Youthful Lesbian —
romantic, idealistic Berrigan.   ISBN 0-941483-55-X   8.95

LESBIANS IN GERMANY by Lillian Faderman & B. Eriksson.
128 pp. Fiction, poetry, essays.   ISBN 0-941483-62-2   8.95

THERE'S SOMETHING I'VE BEEN MEANING TO TELL
YOU Ed. by Loralee MacPike. 288 pp. Gay men and lesbians
coming out to their children.   ISBN 0-941483-44-4   9.95
                                     ISBN 0-941483-54-1   16.95

LIFTING BELLY by Gertrude Stein. Ed. by Rebecca Mark. 104
pp. Erotic poetry.   ISBN 0-941483-51-7   8.95
                                     ISBN 0-941483-53-3   14.95

ROSE PENSKI by Roz Perry. 192 pp. Adult lovers in a long-term
relationship.   ISBN 0-941483-37-1   8.95

AFTER THE FIRE by Jane Rule. 256 pp. Warm, human novel
by this incomparable author.   ISBN 0-941483-45-2   8.95

SUE SLATE, PRIVATE EYE by Lee Lynch. 176 pp. The gay
folk of Peacock Alley are *all cats.*   ISBN 0-941483-52-5   8.95

CHRIS by Randy Salem. 224 pp. Golden oldie. Handsome Chris
and her adventures.   ISBN 0-941483-42-8   8.95

THREE WOMEN by March Hastings. 232 pp. Golden oldie. A
triangle among wealthy sophisticates. ISBN 0-941483-43-6   8.95

RICE AND BEANS by Valeria Taylor. 232 pp. Love and
romance on poverty row.   ISBN 0-941483-41-X   8.95

PLEASURES by Robbi Sommers. 204 pp. Unprecedented
eroticism.   ISBN 0-941483-49-5   8.95

EDGEWISE by Camarin Grae. 372 pp. Spellbinding
adventure.   ISBN 0-941483-19-3   9.95

FATAL REUNION by Claire McNab. 224 pp. 2nd Det. Inspec.
Carol Ashton mystery.   ISBN 0-941483-40-1   8.95

KEEP TO ME STRANGER by Sarah Aldridge. 372 pp. Romance
set in a department store dynasty.   ISBN 0-941483-38-X   9.95

HEARTSCAPE by Sue Gambill. 204 pp. American lesbian in
Portugal.   ISBN 0-941483-33-9   8.95

IN THE BLOOD by Lauren Wright Douglas. 252 pp. Lesbian
science fiction adventure fantasy   ISBN 0-941483-22-3   8.95

THE BEE'S KISS by Shirley Verel. 216 pp. Delicate, delicious
romance.   ISBN 0-941483-36-3   8.95

RAGING MOTHER MOUNTAIN by Pat Emmerson. 264 pp.
Furosa Firechild's adventures in Wonderland.   ISBN 0-941483-35-5   8.95

IN EVERY PORT by Karin Kallmaker. 228 pp. Jessica's sexy,
adventuresome travels.   ISBN 0-941483-37-7   8.95

OF LOVE AND GLORY by Evelyn Kennedy. 192 pp. Exciting
WWII romance.   ISBN 0-941483-32-0   8.95

CLICKING STONES by Nancy Tyler Glenn. 288 pp. Love
transcending time.   ISBN 0-941483-31-2   9.95

SURVIVING SISTERS by Gail Pass. 252 pp. Powerful love
story.   ISBN 0-941483-16-9   8.95

SOUTH OF THE LINE by Catherine Ennis. 216 pp. Civil War
adventure.   ISBN 0-941483-29-0   8.95

WOMAN PLUS WOMAN by Dolores Klaich. 300 pp. Supurb
Lesbian overview.   ISBN 0-941483-28-2   9.95

SLOW DANCING AT MISS POLLY'S by Sheila Ortiz Taylor.
96 pp. Lesbian Poetry   ISBN 0-941483-30-4   7.95

DOUBLE DAUGHTER by Vicki P. McConnell. 216 pp. A Nyla
Wade Mystery, third in the series.   ISBN 0-941483-26-6   8.95

HEAVY GILT by Delores Klaich. 192 pp. Lesbian detective/
disappearing homophobes/upper class gay society.
                                           ISBN 0-941483-25-8   8.95

THE FINER GRAIN by Denise Ohio. 216 pp. Brilliant young
college lesbian novel.   ISBN 0-941483-11-8   8.95

THE AMAZON TRAIL by Lee Lynch. 216 pp. Life, travel & lore
of famous lesbian author.   ISBN 0-941483-27-4   8.95

HIGH CONTRAST by Jessie Lattimore. 264 pp. Women of the
Crystal Palace.   ISBN 0-941483-17-7   8.95

OCTOBER OBSESSION by Meredith More. Josie's rich, secret
Lesbian life.   ISBN 0-941483-18-5   8.95

LESBIAN CROSSROADS by Ruth Baetz. 276 pp. Contemporary
Lesbian lives.   ISBN 0-941483-21-5   9.95

BEFORE STONEWALL: THE MAKING OF A GAY AND
LESBIAN COMMUNITY by Andrea Weiss & Greta Schiller.
96 pp., 25 illus.   ISBN 0-941483-20-7   7.95

WE WALK THE BACK OF THE TIGER by Patricia A. Murphy.
192 pp. Romantic Lesbian novel/beginning women's movement.
                                           ISBN 0-941483-13-4   8.95

SUNDAY'S CHILD by Joyce Bright. 216 pp. Lesbian athletics, at
last the novel about sports. ISBN 0-941483-12-6   8.95

OSTEN'S BAY by Zenobia N. Vole. 204 pp. Sizzling adventure
romance set on Bonaire. ISBN 0-941483-15-0   8.95

LESSONS IN MURDER by Claire McNab. 216 pp. 1st Det. Inspec.
Carol Ashton mystery — erotic tension!. ISBN 0-941483-14-2   8.95

YELLOWTHROAT by Penny Hayes. 240 pp. Margarita, bandit,
kidnaps Julia. ISBN 0-941483-10-X   8.95

SAPPHISTRY: THE BOOK OF LESBIAN SEXUALITY by
Pat Califia. 3d edition, revised. 208 pp. ISBN 0-941483-24-X   8.95

CHERISHED LOVE by Evelyn Kennedy. 192 pp. Erotic
Lesbian love story. ISBN 0-941483-08-8   9.95

LAST SEPTEMBER by Helen R. Hull. 208 pp. Six stories & a
glorious novella. ISBN 0-941483-09-6   8.95

THE SECRET IN THE BIRD by Camarin Grae. 312 pp. Striking,
psychological suspense novel. ISBN 0-941483-05-3   8.95

TO THE LIGHTNING by Catherine Ennis. 208 pp. Romantic
Lesbian 'Robinson Crusoe' adventure. ISBN 0-941483-06-1   8.95

THE OTHER SIDE OF VENUS by Shirley Verel. 224 pp.
Luminous, romantic love story. ISBN 0-941483-07-X   8.95

DREAMS AND SWORDS by Katherine V. Forrest. 192 pp.
Romantic, erotic, imaginative stories. ISBN 0-941483-03-7   8.95

MEMORY BOARD by Jane Rule. 336 pp. Memorable novel
about an aging Lesbian couple. ISBN 0-941483-02-9   9.95

THE ALWAYS ANONYMOUS BEAST by Lauren Wright
Douglas. 224 pp. A Caitlin Reece mystery. First in a series.
ISBN 0-941483-04-5   8.95

SEARCHING FOR SPRING by Patricia A. Murphy. 224 pp.
Novel about the recovery of love. ISBN 0-941483-00-2   8.95

DUSTY'S QUEEN OF HEARTS DINER by Lee Lynch. 240 pp.
Romantic blue-collar novel. ISBN 0-941483-01-0   8.95

PARENTS MATTER by Ann Muller. 240 pp. Parents'
relationships with Lesbian daughters and gay sons.
ISBN 0-930044-91-6   9.95

THE PEARLS by Shelley Smith. 176 pp. Passion and fun in
the Caribbean sun. ISBN 0-930044-93-2   7.95

MAGDALENA by Sarah Aldridge. 352 pp. Epic Lesbian novel
set on three continents. ISBN 0-930044-99-1   8.95

THE BLACK AND WHITE OF IT by Ann Allen Shockley.
144 pp. Short stories. ISBN 0-930044-96-7   7.95

SAY JESUS AND COME TO ME by Ann Allen Shockley. 288
pp. Contemporary romance.   ISBN 0-930044-98-3   8.95

LOVING HER by Ann Allen Shockley. 192 pp. Romantic love
story.   ISBN 0-930044-97-5   7.95

MURDER AT THE NIGHTWOOD BAR by Katherine V.
Forrest. 240 pp. A Kate Delafield mystery. Second in a series.
                                   ISBN 0-930044-92-4   9.95

ZOE'S BOOK by Gail Pass. 224 pp. Passionate, obsessive love
story.   ISBN 0-930044-95-9   7.95

WINGED DANCER by Camarin Grae. 228 pp. Erotic Lesbian
adventure story.   ISBN 0-930044-88-6   8.95

PAZ by Camarin Grae. 336 pp. Romantic Lesbian adventurer
with the power to change the world. ISBN 0-930044-89-4   8.95

SOUL SNATCHER by Camarin Grae. 224 pp. A puzzle, an
adventure, a mystery — Lesbian romance. ISBN 0-930044-90-8 8.95

THE LOVE OF GOOD WOMEN by Isabel Miller. 224 pp.
Long-awaited new novel by the author of the beloved *Patience
and Sarah*.   ISBN 0-930044-81-9   8.95

THE HOUSE AT PELHAM FALLS by Brenda Weathers. 240
pp. Suspenseful Lesbian ghost story. ISBN 0-930044-79-7   7.95

HOME IN YOUR HANDS by Lee Lynch. 240 pp. More stories
from the author of *Old Dyke Tales*. ISBN 0-930044-80-0   7.95

EACH HAND A MAP by Anita Skeen. 112 pp. Real-life poems
that touch us all.   ISBN 0-930044-82-7   6.95

SURPLUS by Sylvia Stevenson. 342 pp. A classic early Lesbian
novel.   ISBN 0-930044-78-9   7.95

PEMBROKE PARK by Michelle Martin. 256 pp. Derring-do
and daring romance in Regency England. ISBN 0-930044-77-0 7.95

THE LONG TRAIL by Penny Hayes. 248 pp. Vivid adventures
of two women in love in the old west. ISBN 0-930044-76-2   8.95

HORIZON OF THE HEART by Shelley Smith. 192 pp. Hot
romance in summertime New England. ISBN 0-930044-75-4   7.95

AN EMERGENCE OF GREEN by Katherine V. Forrest. 288
pp. Powerful novel of sexual discovery. ISBN 0-930044-69-X 9.95

THE LESBIAN PERIODICALS INDEX edited by Claire
Potter. 432 pp. Author & subject index. ISBN 0-930044-74-6 29.95

DESERT OF THE HEART by Jane Rule. 224 pp. A classic;
basis for the movie *Desert Hearts*. ISBN 0-930044-73-8   8.95

SPRING FORWARD/FALL BACK by Sheila Ortiz Taylor.
288 pp. Literary novel of timeless love. ISBN 0-930044-70-3 7.95

FOR KEEPS by Elisabeth Nonas. 144 pp. Contemporary novel
about losing and finding love.   ISBN 0-930044-71-1   7.95

TORCHLIGHT TO VALHALLA by Gale Wilhelm. 128 pp.
Classic novel by a great Lesbian writer.   ISBN 0-930044-68-1   7.95

LESBIAN NUNS: BREAKING SILENCE edited by Rosemary
Curb and Nancy Manahan. 432 pp. Unprecedented autobiographies
of religious life.   ISBN 0-930044-62-2   9.95

THE SWASHBUCKLER by Lee Lynch. 288 pp. Colorful novel
set in Greenwich Village in the sixties.   ISBN 0-930044-66-5   8.95

MISFORTUNE'S FRIEND by Sarah Aldridge. 320 pp. Historical Lesbian novel set on two continents.   ISBN 0-930044-67-3   7.95

A STUDIO OF ONE'S OWN by Ann Stokes. Edited by
Dolores Klaich. 128 pp. Autobiography.   ISBN 0-930044-64-9   7.95

SEX VARIANT WOMEN IN LITERATURE by Jeannette
Howard Foster. 448 pp. Literary history.   ISBN 0-930044-65-7   8.95

A HOT-EYED MODERATE by Jane Rule. 252 pp. Hard-hitting
essays on gay life; writing; art.   ISBN 0-930044-57-6   7.95

INLAND PASSAGE AND OTHER STORIES by Jane Rule.
288 pp. Wide-ranging new collection.   ISBN 0-930044-56-8   7.95

WE TOO ARE DRIFTING by Gale Wilhelm. 128 pp. Timeless
Lesbian novel, a masterpiece.   ISBN 0-930044-61-4   6.95

AMATEUR CITY by Katherine V. Forrest. 224 pp. A Kate
Delafield mystery. First in a series.   ISBN 0-930044-55-X   8.95

THE SOPHIE HOROWITZ STORY by Sarah Schulman. 176
pp. Engaging novel of madcap intrigue.   ISBN 0-930044-54-1   7.95

THE YOUNG IN ONE ANOTHER'S ARMS by Jane Rule. 224 pp. Classic
Jane Rule.   ISBN 0-930044-53-3   9.95

THE BURNTON WIDOWS by Vickie P. McConnell. 272 pp. A
Nyla Wade mystery, second in the series.   ISBN 0-930044-52-5   7.95

OLD DYKE TALES by Lee Lynch. 224 pp. Extraordinary
stories of our diverse Lesbian lives.   ISBN 0-930044-51-7   8.95

DAUGHTERS OF A CORAL DAWN by Katherine V. Forrest.
240 pp. Novel set in a Lesbian new world.   ISBN 0-930044-50-9   8.95

AGAINST THE SEASON by Jane Rule. 224 pp. Luminous,
complex novel of interrelationships.   ISBN 0-930044-48-7   8.95

LOVERS IN THE PRESENT AFTERNOON by Kathleen
Fleming. 288 pp. A novel about recovery and growth.
    ISBN 0-930044-46-0   8.95

TOOTHPICK HOUSE by Lee Lynch. 264 pp. Love between
two Lesbians of different classes.   ISBN 0-930044-45-2   7.95

MADAME AURORA by Sarah Aldridge. 256 pp. Historical
novel featuring a charismatic ''seer.''   ISBN 0-930044-44-4   7.95

CURIOUS WINE by Katherine V. Forrest. 176 pp. Passionate
Lesbian love story, a best-seller.   ISBN 0-930044-43-6   8.95

BLACK LESBIAN IN WHITE AMERICA by Anita Cornwell.
141 pp. Stories, essays, autobiography.   ISBN 0-930044-41-X   7.95

CONTRACT WITH THE WORLD by Jane Rule. 340 pp.
Powerful, panoramic novel of gay life.   ISBN 0-930044-28-2   9.95

MRS. PORTER'S LETTER by Vicki P. McConnell. 224 pp.
The first Nyla Wade mystery.   ISBN 0-930044-29-0   7.95

TO THE CLEVELAND STATION by Carol Anne Douglas.
192 pp. Interracial Lesbian love story.   ISBN 0-930044-27-4   6.95

THE NESTING PLACE by Sarah Aldridge. 224 pp. A
three-woman triangle — love conquers all!   ISBN 0-930044-26-6   7.95

THIS IS NOT FOR YOU by Jane Rule. 284 pp. A letter to a
beloved is also an intricate novel.   ISBN 0-930044-25-8   8.95

FAULTLINE by Sheila Ortiz Taylor. 140 pp. Warm, funny,
literate story of a startling family.   ISBN 0-930044-24-X   6.95

ANNA'S COUNTRY by Elizabeth Lang. 208 pp. A woman
finds her Lesbian identity.   ISBN 0-930044-19-3   8.95

PRISM by Valerie Taylor. 158 pp. A love affair between two
women in their sixties.   ISBN 0-930044-18-5   6.95

THE MARQUISE AND THE NOVICE by Victoria Ramstetter.
108 pp. A Lesbian Gothic novel.   ISBN 0-930044-16-9   6.95

OUTLANDER by Jane Rule. 207 pp. Short stories and essays
by one of our finest writers.   ISBN 0-930044-17-7   8.95

ALL TRUE LOVERS by Sarah Aldridge. 292 pp. Romantic
novel set in the 1930s and 1940s.   ISBN 0-930044-10-X   8.95

A WOMAN APPEARED TO ME by Renee Vivien. 65 pp. A
classic; translated by Jeannette H. Foster.   ISBN 0-930044-06-1   5.00

CYTHEREA'S BREATH by Sarah Aldridge. 240 pp. Romantic
novel about women's entrance into medicine.
        ISBN 0-930044-02-9   6.95

TOTTIE by Sarah Aldridge. 181 pp. Lesbian romance in the
turmoil of the sixties.   ISBN 0-930044-01-0   6.95

THE LATECOMER by Sarah Aldridge. 107 pp. A delicate love
story.   ISBN 0-930044-00-2   6.95

ODD GIRL OUT by Ann Bannon.   ISBN 0-930044-83-5   5.95
I AM A WOMAN 84-3; WOMEN IN THE SHADOWS 85-1;   each

JOURNEY TO A WOMAN 86-X; BEEBO BRINKER 87-8. Golden
oldies about life in Greenwich Village.

JOURNEY TO FULFILLMENT, A WORLD WITHOUT MEN, and   3.95
RETURN TO LESBOS. All by Valerie Taylor   each

These are just a few of the many Naiad Press titles — we are the oldest and
largest lesbian/feminist publishing company in the world. Please request a
complete catalog. We offer personal service; we encourage and welcome direct
mail orders from individuals who have limited access to bookstores carrying
our publications.